My First Real Pash

and Other Stories

My First Real Pash

and Other Stories

Katy Soljak

Press

Published by 99% Press,
an imprint of Lasavia Publishing Ltd.
Auckland, New Zealand
www.lasaviapublishing.com

Copyright © Katy Soljak, 2021
Paintings by Katy Soljak
Back cover picture by Miles Gillett
Photos of paintings by Peter Rees
Cover design and layout by Daniela Gast
Thanks to Susy Hunter and Julie Biuso

ISBN: 978-1-99-115191-9

To my mother, Margaret, who brought us up
with love, patience and a sense of humour.
Mum always loved a good story.

Preface

When I studied at Auckland Teachers' College in 1982, I was fortunate to be taught New Zealand literature under Alan Trussell-Cullen. Having just returned home as a single mother after a decade in the States, it was a welcome homecoming: NZ stories by NZ authors telling their own stories. Alan reminded us to read for our personal enjoyment, *there'll be no time to read for pleasure once you're a teacher*, he'd chuckle.

I began writing my own short stories when I retired from teaching on Waiheke Island in 2008. *My First Real Pash* has been recorded and read on Radio New Zealand by Ginette McDonald with '*He's a Rebel*', by the Crystals as intro and outro. *File This* has also been read on RNZ and published in *Takahe*. *Troy* was published in *Landfall* and some have been published in *Phantom Bill Stickers Café Reader*.

Finally, I'd frame the view
out the front window. At midday
the lawn glitters in the sun
and children fall through time
so quickly, no one can catch them.

From *The Room* by Mary Macpherson

Contents

My First Real Pash

remember my first *real* kiss. It was with Keith Kennedy from Hastings, a stocky swarthy lad who was fifteen and could drive. It happened at the Friday night social at the St. Georges' Church hall in Havelock North. The dress I wore that night was a straight 'A' frame mini with pink, chocolate brown and fawn splotches on a white background. Keith Kennedy asked me to dance and we stayed together all night after that. There wasn't a band, just a record player playing rock n' roll and the top forty hits of the time. *He's A Rebel* by the Crystals was my favourite track and the first forty-five I'd bought with money from babysitting.

Back to Keith. He was sexy. I remember liking his muscular body and strong arms.

I liked his name, Kennedy. We were all still sad about JFK. Keith had driven his father's work truck to the dance. So we danced, glued together like two new shoots in the undergrowth, grooving, moving closely together.

I looked over at my older sister, in her big pink Rock n' Roll skirt with the blow up inner tube petticoat and polka dot poodles. She was earnestly dancing with her new boyfriend Murray, a quiet country lad with fabulous legs. They knew Rock n' Roll dancing, the steps, the twirls. But in this tiny church hall, in this tiny village on the East Coast, Keith and I only had eyes for each other. In between the Troggs' *Wild Thing* and *Peggy Sue*, Keith bought me a Fanta and looked after me.

He told me that he played rugby for the Hastings Boys' High

first fifteen and asked would I like to come to his next game. At precisely 10.00 pm the record player was turned off and the 'Social' was over. The church hall lights were turned up and we found our coats.

'Would you like me to drive you home, Cathy?' Keith asked shyly.

I directed Keith round the bends and turns to Awarua Crescent and he drove carefully in the rusty Bedford with order books and loose bolts strewn across the dashboard. He parked opposite our driveway. I'd already explained about the 2.1 grade and the number of cars that had gotten stuck going up to our place. We listened to the radio. The porch lights at number twelve were still on for us girls coming home. Keith leaned over and attempted some initial pashing, which I responded to with excitement growing inside me, new feelings and all the promise of 'having a boyfriend.' He wanted to go a bit further and I didn't want to be considered 'loose' so I feigned sleep.

'That's right, you go to sleep', he whispered huskily, grappling with my new, white cotton bra. The inside of the cab was steaming up with Keith's enthusiastic advances.

'Cathrine, Cathrine!' It was the unmistakable authoritative voice of my father, standing at the bottom of the driveway, furious.

'I'd better go Keith. It's my Dad'.

'I'll give you a ring.... about the game. We could go to the pictures in town on Saturday, okay?'

I nodded, grabbed my little plastic purse, with my new tangerine swirl lipstick and flew over to the intimidating presence of my father, who'd had a few at the pub. He took me by the left ear and pulled me all the way up the 2.1 driveway. I couldn't look back, but I heard the Bedford crank into gear and knew Keith was making his way back to Hastings, back to his small state house with his dad, where he didn't have a mum and the smell of fried fish and potatoes still hanging in the kitchen air, where he climbed into his single bed with an army wool blanket and his rugby trophies on the dresser.

'Did he make love nicely? My inebriated father muttered sarcastically after me as I made my way down the hallway to my own single bed, shamefully covering my head with the soft eiderdown. I remembered Keith Kennedy's breath, his lips and his voice, 'That's right, go to sleep.'

Saturday morning loomed with its usual burden of chores and never-ending housework. Mum, a reluctant housewife, saved the grubbiest chores for Saturday, when us girls were home from school. I was emptying the ashes from the fireplace into the compost when there was an excited yell from the kitchen window.

'Cathy,' my little sister announced, 'it's a boy on the phone! He wants to talk to you. Ooh you have a boyfriend!'

Feeling the colour burning on my cheeks, I dusted ash off my hands and ran to the phone.

'Can you meet me in town?'

'Yep, no worries, at the bus stop in Heretaunga Street...by the Regent. The game starts at 3.00 pm, okay?'

'Ok, Keith, see you soon.'

Now the difficult part was getting permission to go to the game, something I'd have to negotiate with my mother. She was usually upset and completely dissatisfied by her 'lot' as the wife of a drinking man.

I vacuumed and polished the lounge until the turquoise vinyl couch sparkled and all the ornaments on the mantelpiece shone proudly, each one a tragic reminder of a short holiday stolen between pregnancies and the children's chickenpox.

Finally, I approached the steamy, sweaty cave of the laundry where my mother stooped and scrubbed, tears rolling down her 'English rose' complexion, surrounded by the mountain of never-ending washing.

I stood with determination at the door. 'Mum, can I go to watch a Rugby game in Hastings?'

'What? There's lots more housework to do! How will you get there?' she wiped her brow.

'But I've done all my jobs, you should see the lounge.'

Long sigh.

I didn't wait to hear anymore. I flew to my room and changed quickly into my jeans and a black jumper, leapt on my bike and rode the mile to the village, with a speed that I never knew possible.

On the bus to Hastings, I nervously rolled my bus ticket between my fingers until it crumbled into bits. As the Newman's bus wheezed to a stop by the Regent, Keith shyly approached, dressed for the game in a red and blue rugby jersey and shorts. We hugged awkwardly in the frosty, autumn sun.

'Better get going Cathy, games going to start. Here, I bought this for you,' Keith pressed a bar of dark Nestles chocolate into my hand and took off to join his team.

His Dad and I sat in the stands, with a warm tartan blanket covering our knees.

Mr. Kennedy cheered his son on with: 'Get 'im,' and 'Good on ya!' and 'You beauty!' when Keith scored a try.

Slightly bewildered, and not really that sure about the purpose of scrums and lineouts, I followed his lead and cheered and clapped when he did.

Keith came over at the end of the game, which had been a narrow win for his team. His father shook his hand proudly, eyes glistening. 'Good on ya boy!'

Keith blushed under the mud and sweat left on his face and smiled shyly at me.

'How did you like the game, Cathy?'

'You were really good Keith.'

'Still wanta go to the flicks?'

'Okay'.

He leaned in for a quick kiss and I smelled the earthy sweat of a young aspiring rugby player and felt the warmth of his strong arms around me. Standing there with the damp early evening mist rising up from the field I felt my teenage life was just beginning and that now that I had a boyfriend, things would never be quite the same. I carefully pasted the stubs from the pictures in my diary when I got home and wrote 'K.K XX' next to them.

Some posh Havelock North girls had been at the show that night, the Beatles movie, *A Hard Day's Night.* I had seen them turn back and look at Keith and I, cuddling up in the back row. They had whispered and giggled until the manager told them off.

On Monday at school, Andrea, the leader of the posh group, to which I had tentative membership, condescendingly let me know that the girls thought my new boyfriend, looked a bit 'greasy,' a bit low class.

I didn't belong to the posh group. Economically and socially my parents did not exactly belong to the 'twin set and pearls' crowd. My Mum didn't even drive, let alone play golf or go skiing in winter. But the girls in the 'posh group' tolerated me, were amused and entertained by me. After all, I knew all the words to all the songs in the current Top Twenty and even sang them in tune. They would graciously take turns on my second-hand bike while I would ride their well-groomed horses through the lush

Hawkes Bay countryside.

At school, Andrea often made fun of my shoes, which were definitely an economy line, and my cheap school satchel because it had a handle on the end. 'Look', she'd shriek with laughter, to the girls, 'It has a handle on the end!' But to have them disapprove of my 'greasy' boyfriend, that was unthinkable.

When Keith called the next weekend, I told him that I was too busy to see him, lots of 'swat,' to do for the exams. The next weekend I let my older sister fend off the calls. Keith stopped calling after that and I often wonder what became of him. I haven't seen his name in the All Blacks line-ups and no longer live in the area.

Dating boys from the privileged set had its surprises. I remember young Mr. Campbell, who was not very tall, stretching up to full height in front of my irate father, and telling him a huge lie. My father who was an A-grade mechanic, listened to this trumped-up tale of a broken generator which young Mr. Campbell somehow miraculously fixed in order to bring me home from the date. He made himself sound like a bit of a hero when all along he'd been trying to get to second base with me in the backseat of his VW. It was 3.00 am and my mother stood wretchedly in her candlewick dressing gown. 'We called the hospital and the police.' Her face was puffy from crying. But my father did not overreact. After all this was Mr. Campbell's son, one of the richest farmers in Hawkes Bay.

Rich boys – they would cruise down Heretaunga Street on Friday nights, with their Moleskin trousers, Airtex shirts and their light coloured VWs. Farmers' sons, cruising for girls. They played the field though, stopping into the Intermezzo Coffee lounge for European style coffee and chocolate éclairs, checking out the local girls, much like their well bred fathers would cull the prime cattle in the stock yards. The night's party spot would be whispered, beer was somehow bought, and, if you were lucky enough, you got to go.

They had the pick of the town, but would eventually all marry rich girls from the 'right families.' The reality for girls like me, who were not from the 'right family,' was that we were never taken that seriously. We were not the girls they would take to the ball or skiing to Ruapehu with Mummy and Daddy. Not that different from éclairs really, picked up and enjoyed for the moment. Yes, moneyed families in Hawkes Bay were very strict about who their boys would marry.

I'd like to imagine that Keith Kennedy found a decent girl who loved him for himself and they are now living out their years together with a family. But I also wonder that maybe he was the very essence of a true and decent man, which I in my subsequent pursuit of rebels and bad boys perhaps missed out in ever knowing.

The Social

lied to my diary that night. Wish I still had those diaries but Mum tossed them out along with my Beatles mags when she left Dad. *Danced every dance with Eric. It was soooo romantic.* Lies all lies. The preparation for the end of year social, held at the Anglican Church hall had begun badly. Mum insisted I have a haircut before the big night. 'It's getting untidy, you want to look nice don't you?'

I studied my sandy pageboy intently in the wardrobe mirror, deciding it looked okay, like a surfy chick. My fringe just fell below my eyebrows, *kinda sexy*, I thought.

In retrospect, my mother, having problems with her daughter's development, thought so too, and quickly put an end to that. 'A nice neat haircut should do the trick.'

I was too excited about the upcoming school social to remember that I hardly ever agreed with what my mother considered 'neat' or 'tidy.' Boring and conservative, more like it.

'Just pop into Pam's in the village,' she called after me as I hopped on my bike, 'right after school darling, I made an appointment.'

Liar, liar, pants on fire. Every dance with Eric. He held me close. I could smell his skin, sunlight soap clean.

I parked my bike, a two-tone green second hand job my Dad had restored with a shiny new bell and snappy carrier, against the stucco wall of Pam's pink hair salon. The claustrophobic fumes steaming from old Mrs Simpson's 'do' almost knocked me out as

I snuck into the nearest vinyl chair, all turquoise sparkles, Mum would have loved.

'Won't be two ticks dear. Just a cut today?'

'Yes,' I muttered quietly, not wanting any of the ladies to notice me. They might ask questions. I was shy around strangers in those days.

Pam, her fag dangling dangerously from her frosted pink lips, deftly yanked soggy perm papers from Mrs. Simpson's head. I was faint from the fumes, wishing I could be back on my bike, heading for home or anywhere but Pam's Hair Salon. The village clock chimed five. I was thinking of ways to get out of the dreaded haircut.

'I hear my Mum calling,' I started to mumble.

'Okay dear, come up to the chair. Mrs. Simpson are you happy with that perm? Isn't the blue a perfect shade? Just like the sky. I can't find my glasses anywhere. Have you seen them pet?'

'I told you Mrs. I looked everywhere.' Lorraine, squeezed into a tight white pencil skirt and stilettos, rolled her eyes and continued sweeping up the powder blue curls, making a perfect pile of paper rose petals, on the lilac lino.

So Pam was going to cut my precious shoulder length hair, without her glasses, great!

'Okay then. Sit up straight. No wiggling or I'll cut it crooked and you won't like it,' she crackled followed by a hacking cough.

I already knew I wasn't going to like it if Pam's hair was anything to go on, all teased out, bleached blonde, fifties style. I'd have none of that. My girlfriends and I, all mad on the Beatles, copied their girlfriends' hairstyles: long and straight with heavy fringes.

'Your Mum said you wanted it nice and short for summer.'

'I do?'

'Yes, nice and short. Now where are my glasses? I know they're somewhere around here.' Pam's shears were snipping away and my sandy brown locks were falling to the floor at an alarming speed. 'Nice and short, it'll be easy to keep up after swimming an' that, easy as pie.'

Snip, snip, more hair falling. This time Pam was clipping around my ears. No one had seen those for years. Not that they were abnormal or unpretty. It just wasn't the style. None of the Beatles' girlfriends had short hair, none of them.

'Woops, sorry 'bout that.' Pam's sharp scissors had nipped a piece of my right ear. 'Bit of sticky plaster will sort that out my dear. You'll be right as rain. Bring a plaster Lorraine, chop, chop!'

I couldn't believe the vision of my new 'do' now appearing in the steamy mirror. I looked like a boy, not a twelve-year-old girl about to go to her first social. My heart fell and tears started forming. How could I go now?

'OK, that's good, how do you like it, pet?'

I nodded numbly and headed for the door, the cool breeze from outside blowing against my exposed ears. No more ponytails or pigtails. That was it. I had a boy's haircut.

I rode home with the speed of a mad thing, furious with my mother for causing this to happen right before the social. How could she?

'That looks nice and tidy dear.' Mum was taking the skin off the rice pudding.

'Nice and tidy, nice and tidy, who wants to be nice and tidy? I hate this bloody haircut. It's the worst cut I've ever seen. I'll never be able to go to the social like this Mum. How could you?'

'Well, some gratitude, I shouldn't have bothered.' Mum closed the oven door with more force than was needed and wiped her brow.

'I know, we could give her a perm, Mum.' My older sister Susan looked up from her teen mag, smiling. Was this a plot to make me look completely ridiculous?

Before I could protest the two of them were fixing curlers and perm papers with all the speed of professionals. Now I smelled just like old Mrs. Simpson.

'It's a Toni home perm sis, you won't be able to tell the difference from the salon once we're done,' Susan chuckled. 'Which twin has the Toni?'

Why was I trusting these two? It was obvious we had completely different taste in everything. Susan loved Elvis. I hated Elvis. I loved the Beatles and Bob Dylan. Mum said he sounded like he was dying.

'I've picked out something for you to wear tonight dear.' God, how bad could this get? 'You remember that box of clothes from your cousins in Auckland?'

'Mmmm.'

'Well there's a lovely paisley shirt frock, pleated, very nice. It'll be perfect for your social.'

Numb, I was becoming numb from the base of the curlers through to my toes, numb. 'What colour is it Mum?'

'Oh you know, earthy tones.'

Earthy tones, shirt frock? Patty Boyd wouldn't be seen dead in an earthy toned shirt frock. God, couldn't Mum ever get it?

'How long does this stinky perm take Mum? I have to be at the hall at 7.00 pm sharp.' I tried to sound firm. They weren't listening anyway.

'Ooh this curler is loose here at the neck Mum, better redo it eh?'

Somehow I arrived at the entrance of the hall, my plate of soggy pikelets and jam in hand. I could see the popular girls' group, of which I was a fringe member, gather in a conspiratorial coven when they saw my apparition in the doorway, my head crowned in a halo of tight Toni curls, giggling and pointing. I managed to squeeze past them to sit on the hard wooden bench on the right side of the musty hall, boys on the left. My eyes focused on the floor in front of me for the first few dances, watching for the shoes of a potential 'dance date.'

The wallflowers and I waited through the *Twist*, by Chubby Checker, looking up from time to time to watch the popular group work their lithe successful hips into a frenzy. Their page boys coiffed and sprayed with a soft mist of Sunsilk, flying in and out with each twist, Jackie headbands like triumphant banners, splashing pastel colours into the pale room.

'Did you get a home perm?' A breathless Abigail inquired, flinging her pretty polka-dot skirts on to the bench space beside me.

'Mum did it,' I monotoned into the floor.

She giggled into her pink hanky, 'That Charles is soo naughty. He keeps trying to dance too close.'

Abigail's laugh rang out as the rest of the popular group swarmed in and gathered her up in a swirl of pink poplin and Morny June Rose. 'C'mon, Abigail. The boys said we should all get some Fanta.'

The breeze from their collective spring frocks flew around my still numbness and was gone, leaving me alone in between 'Frog Eyes' and 'Fleabag,' who nobody ever talked to.

I moved further down the bench, closer to the wall, hoping I could meld into it and disappear. The supper call shrilled out: three whistles from Miss Gilbert, the Phys Ed teacher. The popular group swished and flurried about, giggling, pinkies up, serviettes and orange fizzy drinks. We, the girls who didn't fit in, sat woodenly, immobilized.

'*Tonight your mine completely,*' the Shirelles sang out from Miss Gilbert's portable stereogram and the second half began. The three of us on the bench, watched the popular boys comb their hair and swagger over to the popular girls, choosing their favourite dance partners. I picked harder at the seam in my shirtdress. '*One for the money, two for the show, three to get ready,*' squeals as the boys swung their eager prizes side to side.

'*Don't you step on my blue suede shoes,*' sang out. The popular girls' black patent leather shoes winked cheekily. '*Ally oop oop oop oop oop*', a spontaneous Congo line snaked by, weaving delirious, popular petticoats crackling and poking our knees.

'Stop it Charles!' squealed Abigail.

'Leap Year dance boys and girls,' announced Miss Gilbert on the loud hailer. 'Girls, choose your partners for the last dance'.

I rose slowly from the bench, pins and needles tingling in my toes, which had been squeezed inside my sister's slip-ons for two and a half hours. My walk across to the boys' side felt like slow motion.

'Wanna have this dance?' I mumbled to Eric, who blushed red. I'd noticed he'd been sitting out a few. He rose politely and we walked out on the dance floor. Eric shyly took my hand in his, sweaty and trembling, and we attempted a slow waltz to, *Going to the Chapel.*

My eyes focused down on Eric's polished shoes. 'One two three, One two three,' I could hear him whispering.

'I didn't recognize you tonight,' he noted quietly,' you look so different. Have you done something with your hair?'

I nestled into the sunlight soap smell of his ironed white dress shirt and closed my eyes.

'*And we'll never be lonely anymore...*'

Spitting Image

hat ya doin' Dad ?'

'You'll see. It's a surprise. Pass me that rag by the paint tin, Kitty.' Dad's hand reached down and picked up the old faded nappy. He looked taller than five-eleven, way up top of the old wooden ladder.

'What ya painting up there?'

'You'll see.' He smiled down, a benevolent giant, the Havelock sun crowning his dark, wavy hair. 'You'll see when it's done.'

By late afternoon, a small gathering of neighbourhood kids had assembled like curious ants at the base of the ladder, peering up at the sign above the gardening shed. He'd been at it all afternoon and the old shed walls were now fresh with a new coat of flat black. He'd taken out the window and built a small shelf in front.

'What's ya Dad doin'?'

'I don't know, it's a surprise.'

'Weeeeooooeeew!'

'We gotta go, that's Mum's whistle, see ya tomorrow, okay?' The two Dutch girls from next door, scrambled over the fence as fast as ferrets. The older one, Jolie, getting her summer frock caught in the fence wire.

'Oh, no! Mum's gonna give me a hiding. I've ripped it.' She ran crying home to her mother's spotless living room, carefully taking off her leather sandals at the door. Those girls weren't allowed to play inside so they came over to our place. It was more fun they said. Their mother whistled them home for tea and often yelled out at full volume, for them to come home to do their 'bollies' and 'vee vees.'

'Come in for your tea girls!' Mum was standing at the back door, the baby on her hip. 'When are you coming in Fred? Dinner's ready.' She jiggled the baby and straightened her floral pinny.

'Soon as I finish,' Dad yelled back.

'When will that be? Tea's getting cold.'

Dad didn't answer, but went on painting, ignoring her.

Mum sighed and smoothed a strand of blonde hair back behind her ear. 'C'mon girls, wash your hands.'

'What's Dad making anyway?' Shirley, the oldest sister, sipped her cold glass of milk at the grey formica table, looking up from the rock n' roll mag she was drooling over. She was mad about Elvis and thought we were immature and annoying.

'We don't know Shirl. Pass the butter.'

We were starving. The lamb chops, mashed spuds and green beans from the garden were disappearing fast. Mum fed the baby, looking out the window. We were hoeing into our Edmonds custard and peaches when Dad's tall frame darkened the kitchen door.

'Okay kids, you can see now. She's all done.' He wiped his brow with a rag and smiled his famous white teeth smile with the splash of gold.

'Not now, Fred. They haven't finished their pudding.' Long sigh.

We tore past her and ran outside into the dark backyard.

'There you go Kitty, your own shop!' He shone his torch over to the chook house and next to it we could see the sign, 'KITT'S BONZA STORE,' painted in tall black bold letters on a white background, above the shed. 'Come on, have a look!'

'Gosh, is that for me Dad?'

'Your own little shop, just for you dear.'

My sister Annie looked down and blushed. No wonder she often felt like the third wheel.

'You can play in it too,' I assured her, putting my big sister arm around her.

'Look at this girls.' He went inside the 'shop' and pulled down the black blind, which said, *closed.*

I loved it, Kitt's Bonza Store, my own shop!

It was the hit of the neighbourhood. Kids from all round the crescent streamed over to play shop that summer of '59. The plastic cash register Santa had been kind enough to give me, rang out and all the kids went home with empty sellotaped packets of Rinso and Sunlight soap. But they had to give back the shiny play money change, before they left.

I was always the shopkeeper, of course, but I would let Annie relieve me when I had to go to the toilet. The change in the till was counted with precision upon my return and I insisted she keep all the cartons straight and orderly on the shelves. There were also repairs to do on the cartons and we went through lots of tape.

When Mum called us in for tea, I would sweep out the shop and pull down the *closed* sign with pride.

Aunty Nola was over visiting Mum that summer. She wasn't our real aunty. 'She's such a character!' Mum would say. She was really the exact opposite of our blonde, educated and well-spoken mother. Nola was pretty in a tarty sort of way, with her tight 'peddle pushers' and bold print blouses. She was like a small town Connie Francis, sitting at our kitchen table, with her plucked eyebrows and black shiny curls. She would show up with her brood on the weekends in her red Austin 1100 and keep Mum in fits all afternoon, telling rude jokes and smoking menthols.

Dad would come home and join in the merriment. They'd sip sherry in the front room and hoot loudly at Shelley Berman LPs. Dad would disconnect the speaker in the kitchen so we couldn't hear the racy jokes, but we would sneak a listen at the door anyway.

Aunty Nola's kids, two dark curly haired girls around my age, and a younger blonde haired boy, were very impressed with Kitt's Bonza Store. I let the oldest girl Nicky, try out the cash register, only because she was the most responsible, and we'd play shops all afternoon. The Dutch girls were our main customers. They didn't have anywhere else to go, being shut outside as usual. It was fast trading all day with short runs inside the house for cold lemonade.

'Gosh, I wish our Dad would make us a shop,' Nicky sighed,' He's always working.'

Years later, when I was 30 something, divorced and home from overseas with my own young children, Aunty Nola's boy, Bevan, paid my sister Annie and I a visit.

We were sharing a classic old bungalow in Takapuna, with wooden panelled walls and stained glass windows. Our kids loved the big backyard, full of old fruit trees with branches that spread out like bony arms. We were so surprised to see him after all that time. Annie had always liked him. They'd had a bit of a crush on each other as kids, both blondies. I'd taken after my dad with brown hair and all my sisters were blondes like Mum. Our Nana, dad's Mum was also a white blonde with great legs. I used to say I was adopted. Mum would laugh and say, 'No chance of that Kitty, you're the spitting image of your father.' *Spitting image*, I couldn't fathom that expression. Why say 'spit,' it was rude wasn't it? Bevan was tall now, close to six foot, grown up with his own family and eager to rekindle our childhood friendship. He arrived alone, with pastries and photos, all smiles, tanned, his blonde hair smoothed back.

'Great to see you again Bevan, what's the occasion?' Annie was curious.

'Wait till the kids finish their snack and I'll tell ya.' He flashed us a big smile.

'Go and play outside kids.' I shooed them all outside. The cousins never tired of playing go-home-stay-home on the green grass out back. The trees were perfect hiding places.

Over fresh ground coffee, Bevan told us his news. 'Well, girls, the truth is, I have good reason to believe I'm your brother, or half brother.'

'What?' I was stunned.

'Go on,' said Annie, her blue eyes shining. She loved a good story.

'Yes, well, my Dad, Harry, was going into hospital for a triple bypass a few months back and he had a quiet word with me, the night before the op. "Son, I just want you to know, if I don't pull through this, there's something you should know. I'm not your real father. I've loved you and raised you as my own but the truth is, you're not my son."'

'Wow!' we sat back from the table, incredulous.

'Yeah, well I asked Dad who my real father was and he said he couldn't tell me that for sure but he'd heard through the grapevine that Nola had been having an affair with your dad when he and Mum were separated. Mum was preggers when they got back together a year later, and, when I was born he raised me as his own son. I remember playing on my bike one day, and the neighbour next door, who didn't like mum, was talking over the fence to a lady. "There goes that Traffic cop's kid," she said. I don't look anything like my sisters. Mum and Dad also have black hair and brown eyes.'

Annie and I studied Bevan's face. God, his blue eyes were exactly the same colour as our father's. One eye was slightly smaller than the other, with crow's feet starting to show just like his had.

'Mum won't tell me the truth,' he went on. 'Reckon she's gonna take that one to the grave. We never really got along. She was always closer to the girls. Dad worked a lot with his business and wasn't home much. I guess I was a bit of a hell raiser, hard to handle.'

For once in our lives my sister and I were speechless. It seemed incredible that the little blonde boy we'd played chasing and shops with that summer, was actually our own brother. We'd always wanted a brother. Mum had lost a boy baby. He was stillborn after Annie. We'd always felt that something was missing after that.

Squeals of laughter outside broke the silence as the cousins' chasing game continued. The afternoon sun was turning rosy peach and the kitchen clock ticked away.

'That's right,' Annie remembered, 'Dad used to spend the odd weeknight down in Taradale. Something about traffic officer training I think Mum said.'

'Yeah, well, Nola ran a little bottle-shop business in front of our place and your dad would often come round and have a few sherries with the old girl. I remember him ruffling my hair a few times and throwing me up in the air. Look here's some old photos of us growing up. Here's Nicky and sis and there's me, don't look anything like them do I?'

We pored over the faded black and white Brownie shots, very like our own collection in Mum's leather suitcase. Kids standing in order of size on their front steps, squinting from the sun, forced smiles.

'What's this?' I picked one up, taken in *their* backyard. In the forefront, Bevan smiling shyly in a towelling short set and in the background, what looked like a small black shed. His two dark haired sisters stood at attention in front of it. Above them in black and white letters the hand painted sign read, KITT'S BONZA STORE.

Troy

roy and Brandon were coming over to the island for the weekend. I hadn't seen them in months. They were both artists living in one of Kingsland's remaining shop fronts. You never knew what would happen with Troy. She once told me how she liked stumbling around at night. She'd stumble home from a night's dancing and carousing at Java Jive, sweetly numb and teetering in her black Mini Coopers, worn down at the heels, her frantic mohair sweater in twisted abstract shades of autumn, pulled down over her tight, black leather skirt. She glowed boldly in the yellow lights of Ponsonby. Troy liked dancing with women when she was like that.

'Slowly, slowly,' she'd say, leading them like a man, slowing their earnest moves down to a sensuous groove. 'Slowly,' she'd whisper in their ear. Then she'd laugh, finding it amusing that her nervous dance partner, being straight, was aroused and giving into her lead.

Pedro was leaving for Greece to work on an asparagus sorter. It was going to be a big bash. We all crowded into Geoffrey's new white people mover while Brandon taught us all the 'Bogun rebel yell.' We shouted it out that night in the all-white room, with floors like marble and thick plastered walls, like in Greece.

'Yip, yip, yip, yeaooooaaahhheeee!' We all tried our best, got our bodies into it. It was good to be bogun. 'Yip, yip, yip, yeaaaahhhh.' Our voices echoed back off the plaster walls.

In the midst of the wicked Bogun group, wildly dancing to the

Doors, *Break on Through to the Other Side*, I let loose and boogied like a wild woman. It was in that moment, spying through the thick glass door, that I saw Troy taking Geoffrey's hand, on the suede couch.

'Hold my hand preacher man,' she whispered.

He being hard of hearing, lent in closer to hear her soft cupie doll lips pouting, her sleepy eyes lowering.

'Hold my hand,' Troy cooed.

They sat like that amidst the noise of the night, with people blah, blah, blahing on all sides and Troy dozing off the lazy dinner rosé. *My Geoffrey* holding hands, smiling and frozen, like a lovesick teenager with *cupie doll* Troy, nestling into the comfort of his soft leather jacket, her blonde sausage curls tumbling down his beating chest.

How would you like me to hold hands and snuggle with someone like that?

Brandon and naughty Troy slept off the Waiheke wine at the local backpackers and arrived at our place too late for brekkie. The buckwheat pancakes I'd flipped for them, now hard and lonely in the oven.

'We've come to do your portraits, remember?' she teased.

Brandon stood shyly at the door behind her. His arms full of large rolls of drawing paper rolled up in a tube while his strong Irish hands clutched freshly sharpened drawing pencils. It was a far cry from the happy Bogun yeller, careening down Shelley Beach Road at 2.00 am, smashing into the mirror of a small Toyota and stumbling towards the ditch laughing, a wild midnight jester.

Troy directed the portraits while her man sketched Geoffrey, his brown hands skillfully moving over the paper, liquid, smooth.

'You won't like them,' she giggled, her blonde curls quivering. 'They're never flattering. Honestly, you'll *hate* them!'

Geoffrey, now a pathetic pawn in her game, sat upright, obedient in his black Adidas tracksuit with all his TV remotes laid out on his stiff knees, seven altogether.

'Remote man! Techie man!' Troy was ecstatic.

It was a good likeness. Geoffrey's expression, slightly worried, *It takes a worried man...* The remotes were practically falling to the floor, lines swirled around his feet like a whirlpool, his back strong.

Troy called from the city later that week and confessed. 'We can't go back to that Irish pub. The manager woman told us we were too loud, too unruly! Not very Irish.' That giggle. She told me how she'd crawled on her hands and bloodied knees up the hill from Molly Malone's.

Their last night, on the island, she'd stumbled in her high red velvet hoochie Mama shoes and fallen down a ditch. Drunk on Irish whiskey, she'd cracked her slim ankle. Blue and swollen, it had to be set in plaster when they got back to Auckland.

Brandon, the romantic, had proposed to her on the ferry home. He'd bought her red roses and dropped the scented petals into the froth from the propellers.

'Yes!' She'd said happily, giddy from Lindauer, 'Yes!'

Hold my hand preacher man, a quiet voice inside my head.

I offer congratulations and say goodbye.

You never knew what would happen with Troy.

The Family Gold

he push up to the Fitzroy Wharf was perhaps a little too rough, more like a shove from behind. Maggie lost her balance on the rusty ladder rungs and felt her knee graze as she grappled with her Nike bag and pulled herself on to dry land.

'Here.' Richard passed up her guitar, squinting in the sharp December sun. That was all he said as he descended quickly into the inflatable dinghy and buzzed back to his yacht. She was beautiful, a Classic, like an elegant swan with dark mahogany on the deck and around the portholes.

Maggie had been looking forward to them being away together. Three weeks alone on the water by Great Barrier Island, away from their demanding jobs, time to relax and 'play house' on board Richard's yacht. But after only three days at sea it had all gone horribly wrong. On their last night she had crawled into one of the single berths and slept alone. They had barely been speaking to each other and she couldn't understand why.

The pictures they'd taken during Christmas dinner on board showed a happy couple, slightly sunburned and rosy from shiraz. Maggie had proudly served a plump chicken, with her mother's stuffing, baked potatoes, kumara and steamed green beans. For dessert she'd made steamed Christmas pudding, custard and whipped cream. She had bought Christmas presents for the yacht: African woven baskets laden with fresh oranges that swung gently with the motion and complimented the tapa cushion covers in the dining area. The earthy Pacific patterns brought out the rich wood in the galley, it was something she'd done for him before their trip away. She had bought them both matching Chinese silk robes for Christmas, in contrasting shades of blue. Hers was turquoise and Richard's was royal navy blue.

After Christmas dinner he'd grown sullen and uncommunicative, suddenly leaving the table and heaving himself into the cabin. Moments later she heard him snoring, lights out, 'good night nurse,' as he would say. She looked at the Christmas presents he'd given her and felt like throwing them overboard. Two glass coffee cups in metal holders, like something you'd give a neighbour or teacher. It was just not very romantic. *How had it suddenly all changed?*

Now he was shoving her off, sending her back like an unwanted item, no guarantee, return to sender. She would have to take the island ferry back to Auckland, a slow rolling five-hour trip. What would she tell her family? Mother, who thought Richard was marvellous, was already planning her wedding outfit.

She had left the table as it was and taken her coffee out on to the deck, watching the night sky. The Barrier was breathtaking at night. They were anchored in the Fitzroy Harbour and she could hear the easy laughter of other yacht couples enjoying the end of their evening meals, their gaiety rippling out like happy little waves in the moonlit bay. Maggie had felt sad and suddenly quite cold. Coffee cups? She had been hoping for something more special. Jewelry perhaps? And why was he being so distant?

There had been signs. Richard had been unavailable lately and someone called Susan had been over visiting when she'd called last week.

'Business,' he'd said, 'Susan's helping with P.R.'

'She's great, you'll like her,' he said casually over dinner. He'd gone on to say how Susan was wonderfully organized. How she'd brought a basket of freshly baked blueberry muffins down to his yacht for a meeting with clients.

'They don't make women like that anymore,' Maggie had commented dryly.

'She's got a cute new Mazda sports, metallic blue, terrific little car, great mileage,' he added, 'you'd look good in one.'

He squinted at her. There had been signs.

Later Richard had announced that his yacht would be 'Mother Ship' this year, for the annual classic yacht race, from the Ponsonby Cruising Club in Westhaven to Kawau Island.

'Susan will most likely be sailing back with us, you'll meet her then,' Richard had said cheerily. 'She's been on yachts since she was a *chaild*.'

Maggie had noticed a skip in his step as he got up to freshen their glasses.

The race to Kawau Island took off with a sharp pistol crack and the fine lined classics sped past the entrance to Westhaven, fluffing out their sails like pretty birds, pushing forward into the blue Waitemata Harbour. Richard's yacht was up with the rest of them, the early morning light splashing off the polished bow, his face, rosy and excited. He always looked handsome at the helm with his cap and beard. Rather like a well-fed Sean Connery, Maggie thought.

Whoosh! Maggie's cap blew off and sailed into the sea. A cheeky blue ball cap she'd bought back from East Los Angeles, the slogan, 'Mi Vida Loca', My Crazy Life, often felt appropriate.

'God, oh well, there goes that memory.' She laughed up at the skipper.

Richard slowly swung the yacht right round and cleverly

caught the little cap with a long boat hook, before it sank.

'Silly, you'll lose the race now,' she called out over the sea spray.

'Milady shall have her hat!' He handed Maggie the soggy cap with a bow. He could be so charming.

Richard's boat limped in with the last few and much partying and revelry followed at Kawau Bay, 'an excuse for a piss-up,' Maggie noted. Rum flowed, and Susan, well rounded and thoroughly enjoying her hostess role, busied round the sweaty yachties, with trays of perfectly placed hors d'oeuvres, crab cakes, pâté, celery sticks and more of her perfect muffins. Maggie wondered where she'd managed to make them all.

One of the classic lads, who'd had a few rums, gossiped to Maggie about Susan's fling with the champion yacht's captain, a tall sandy-haired 'very married' thirty something, with piercing blue eyes. *So she's not such a proper little lady after all, sleeps with married men*, Maggie thought, watching her flirt with all the yachties, her neck thrown back like a pale bird.

As night fell Susan gathered her belongings from the winning yacht and came aboard Richard's. He brought out a bottle of Baileys from his well-stocked liquor cabinet and the three of them sat around the tapa dining area, sipping the creamy liquor. Maggie was tired and a bit over the 'yachtie' talk, which she didn't really understand, or find that exciting. She excused herself, preparing to bunk down, thinking Richard would follow. She woke an hour or so later and heard them still talking quietly. *There were signs.*

Susan bounced into the galley in the morning, announcing she would be making breakfast. Blonde and bubbly, she'd bought a new omelette flipper and was dying to try it out.

'Such a good deal at Smith and Caugheys! Mummy and I *love*

their sales,' she gushed.

Richard slyly admired this new kitchen bitch, resplendent in her bright white t-shirt, barely covering her tight undies, hugging the top of her chubby thighs.

Maggie thought it was all a bit cheeky: the omelette maker, the way she'd taken over the galley and those white undies, like a schoolgirl's. Richard however, seemed delighted to have Susan onboard, making a huge fuss over the rather soggy plain ham omelette. Maggie thought she'd rather over-steamed it. The yacht race was all over but somebody was still competing for first place.

Richard had recently given Maggie a golden chain with a piece of his 'family gold', dangling like a promise, a tiny misshapen island of ore. He had presented it to her the night of the opera, *Turandot*, arriving at her tiny garret precisely at 6.00 pm in a handsome tux. Cleanly shaven, shoes polished, he presented her with the necklace, fixing it around her neck, claiming her like a prize.

Maggie had gone to some trouble herself and had borrowed a slender red sleeveless gown from her sister. She'd had her auburn hair done up at the hairdresser's and looked elegant.

'I like seeing our family gold around your neck,' he said quietly.

The 'family gold' glistened at her neck and she felt rather like the main character from *Pretty Woman* as she stepped into his black town car.

They clinked chilled glasses of Bollinger at the house of an old friend of Richard's in Ponsonby. Patrick's townhouse was minimal, rather New York, with white brick walls and faux fur throws on real leather couches. Maggie enjoyed the banter of the two old friends and the champers.

'Don't look now, ex-wives in the mezzanine,' the two chaps chuckled like co-conspirators as they entered the Aotea theatre.

Richard would mention his ex on occasion and often grew moody, grieving their recent separation. He was very close to his daughter, Ophelia, and had introduced her proudly to Maggie at a brunch in Kingsland before Christmas.

'Daddy tells me you're a blues-singer.'

'Well I do have a day job also, teaching,' Maggie felt she was being interviewed.

'What do they say? Those that can, do; those who can't, teach. Is that right Daddy?' Ophelia offered her hand, appearing cultured with a private school accent, self-assured, spoiled and definitely 'Daddy's girl.' Richard had wanted a son but that was one deal that had not gone through.

The fabulously planned night at the Opera ended horribly just like their romance. It all changed when Richard and Maggie were having a nightcap on Ponsonby Road after dropping Patrick off.

'Did you see all those people looking at you talking to the Shortland Street actor?'

Maggie hadn't really noticed. *She rolled her eyes.*

Richard was on a roll. 'How do you think I pull off my hundred thousand dollar deals, darling? It's all about putting the right people together at the right time! Timothy could be good for your career. He loves the Blues. That's why I set it all up, had him sit with us.' He was puffed up with pride like a rather tipsy penguin in his smart tux.

'I thought we were out for a romantic night at the Opera,' Maggie said quietly, blowing the froth from her Irish coffee. Somehow she now felt like a pawn and the night seemed like some script he'd written.

Richard became enraged, stormed up to the bar and paid the tab.

He does not respond well to criticism, Maggie noted.

'I'll take you home.' He swung open the door of his waiting Mercedes and almost pushed her in. The huge car was careening too fast down Ponsonby Road.

'Don't bother,' Maggie shouted, 'just drop me off at Java Jive!' She could be contrary too.

'Java Jive, it's always bloody Java Jive!'

He was furious, driving recklessly, weaving the big town car through the night traffic and screeching to a stop outside the bar.

Maggie carefully gathered the folds of her gown off the front seat and slammed the heavy car door a little too hard. Close to tears but not letting them fall, Maggie ordered a flat white sitting alone in all her opera splendour at the bar, her red gown crushing up next to some crusty bar fly. She had so wanted permanence with a good man. Why couldn't she have that? Richard had talked about a future together, about going to live in Melbourne. When they'd first met she found him too enthusiastic and kept him at bay. She'd always been so independent and liked being her own woman. But really she wasn't that different from most women she knew. She wanted someone who loved her completely, was there for her, in her court. In return she would do the same, help her man achieve his goals, love him completely, faithfully.

In the past Maggie had chosen foolishly: younger men with talent. She could always see their potential, though none of her friends ever could. She ignored their weak points, like no money, no car, or often no job, and focused on bringing out their talents. They were never the kind of men she could take home to meet her parents.

Always benefitting from her nurturing, her handsome lovers got on their feet and moved on, leaving her with phone bills and rent to pay.

Richard was different. He had a lot to offer. He was presentable and he listened to her dreams, spoiled her and made her feel beautiful. For the first night they'd spent together at his all white Herne Bay apartment, he'd bought a queen sized bed with new Egyptian linen and white lace pillowcases. On the bed was a gift box wrapped in gold paper with a silk ribbon.

'It's for you Dahling', Richard had whispered in her ear.

Maggie had unwrapped the gold ribbon and the white tissue revealed a lacy black suspender belt, a matching lace bra and sexy black stockings. They'd both enjoyed the feel of the new ensemble inside the fresh linen. She was very quickly becoming used to his style, very black-and-white and always quality. She was developing real feelings for him and often thought about how their future might be together. She'd never known such a romantic gentleman.

Sipping the coffee Maggie thought about all the trouble Richard had gone to for the opera and felt bad. She caught a taxi to his apartment and found him in a dark mood. His white dress shirt was unbuttoned and the tie thrown on the table, the rum bottle drained.

'I've thrown the bloody thing out the window!'

'What?' Maggie was worried.

'The bloody stereo system you said was shit.'

'Oh really?' Maggie was impressed. The stereo really had sucked with its tiny speakers and thin tone.

In the morning over the traditional tea, toast and marmalade he said, 'How could I be mad at you Dahling, showing up at my door in that red gown?'

Yes, it was a glamorous door Richard had opened for her and had now, on that moonlit summer night in Fitzroy Harbour, closed, rudely in her face. Maggie scaled back into the comfort of her bohemian lifestyle and poetry readings on Wednesday evenings and dinner at friends' houses resumed. She threw herself into her work at school. It helped to keep busy.

'What happened to your rich boyfriend?' David, her teaching colleague asked curiously in the staffroom. He'd noticed the steady stream of delicious bouquets flowing past his window over the last few months. Gorgeous bouquets of white orchids and gardenias, the heady perfume filling up the stark little prefab, bringing old world glamour into the room. *Ooooh, Miss has a boyfriend!* the children would chorus.

'I don't know,' Maggie sipped her instant coffee, 'It seems to be all over.'

She didn't want to admit to herself how much she was missing Richard. How her life that she'd always enjoyed, now seemed empty without him. There had been no communication from him for weeks. His home phone was continuously on answer phone and so was his mobile.

Then without warning on a rainy day in early March, Richard showed up at her garret flat in Kingsland with a bottle of genuine French champagne.

'Happy Birthday,' he poured her a glass sheepishly. *Was this an apology for the shabby ending? It was amazing he even remembered.* She offered him a glass.

'No, not for me, I'm not drinking,' he announced proudly. 'Yes, Ai'm on the straight and narrow, given it all up, all of it. It's all coming off, all this weight! Ai've been working out with a trainer. Ai'm going more conservative, dating more conservative women these days.'

'Thanks for sharing,' Maggie muttered. *Susan, it had to be her.* She couldn't see any change in his paunch either, and he now reminded her of Toad from Toad Hall.

She'd always known he'd been into taking speed, not your lowlife street variety, his was 'designer speed' for executives, available, apparently, from his neighbourhood doctor. They were time release capsules, guaranteeing hourly bursts of chemical energy. His days had always seemed hectic.

'Meetings, meetings, back to back all day!' He'd relate to her after work, splashing generous measures of rum into his glass, a comedown tonic from the speed. She'd often expressed her concern for his health with this dangerous combination. So he was giving it all up. Why now?

They small talked about work but she was too hurt and confused to really say what she was feeling. She wanted to let fly with the anger that was still buried inside. She wanted to hurt him, but he'd remembered her birthday. She couldn't spoil that.

It was the last time they would be alone together.

A week later, Maggie was eating an early dinner in Herne Bay, with her friend, Julio, an Argentinean actor. She noticed two old friends of Richard's, sitting at a table for four at the rear of the restaurant. They waved limply when they recognized her. Julio had been catching up with all Maggie's gossip and was laughing when around the corner bounced Richard and Susan in matching blue turtlenecks and conservative slacks. They froze mid-stride upon seeing her. Maggie was speechless. Richard blushed and attempted a lame greeting. He'd met Julio at a housewarming party they'd gone to at David's. Susan was triumphant and gripped her 'prize' firmly in her well-fed hand.

'Looks like he's got himself a breeder,' Julio whispered, watching as the two lovebirds joined their friends, cheek kisses all round.

A few months later, Maggie was playing a gig at the Temple Café in upper Queen Street. She noticed Ophelia cruise in to the packed-out bar during her last set, wearing tight jeans and a black biker jacket.

'Isn't it marvellous Maggie?' Ophelia's eyes sparkled, sidling up to her as she came off stage. 'Have you been invited to Daddy's engagement party?'

Maggie stood still, the roar of the Temple Café whirling around her in slow motion. She managed to shake her head slowly.

'Oh, too bad. It's a black tie affair, but that's soo Daddy! Oh sorry, didn't you know? He's marrying Susan,' she went on excitedly, 'she's loaded. Her daddy's a property developer, multimillionaire or something. It's all so sudden. I think she's pregnant!' she giggled.

'No, they don't make women like that anymore,' Maggie said quietly, packing up her guitar. 'Your daddy sure knows how to close a deal,' she threw back over her shoulder, making her way into the bustle of Queen Street on Friday night.

So, she's loaded, a yachtie and a breeder. Yes, Susan was definitely a 'Super Package Deal,' Maggie thought.

This time she didn't hold back. The bus ride down K' Road seemed surreal through her tears and she didn't care what anyone around her thought. She was hurt and more alone than she could ever remember. The garish streetlights flashed by like coloured streaks. Maggie stumbled off at her stop feeling like a refugee, aching for her homeland.

It was on Bastille Day when Maggie finally disposed of the 'Family Gold.' It no longer felt smooth but rather clung on as a daily reminder of Richard's betrayal.

She'd decided to gamble it away carelessly and only got $50

for it at 246 Jewellers on Queen Street. She marched into the Queen's Head Tavern loading the whole lot on a likely 'pokie': The Chameleon. She watched as the lines quickly lit up and she gambled twenty lines at ten bets a line while sipping on a small bottle of Lindauer, French Champagne being a bit over her budget these days. The seductive tunes on the pokie started up and she won some, then, just as quickly lost it all. Laughing at her own foolishness, she strolled out into the warm sun to spend the day with a faithful old friend on Waiheke Island. In honour of Bastille Day she bought a loaf of French bread and a bottle of cheap red from the Family Barrow, and continued her own private freedom march, singing aloud, *Alons enfants de la Patrie, le jour de gloire est arrive...*

Queensbury Rules at the Baron's Lunch

he setting is the Baron's newly mown front lawn on a balmy island afternoon. Some of our characters straddle the Baron's outdoor furniture, hand-chiselled wooden table and benches, under the shade of pongas and flowering tee tree. Monarch butterflies swoop lightly around the swan plants and tuis call to each other in the karaka tree above: Halcyon summer days.

Edwin, the Baron's boating mate, is hovering inside the kitchen, watching him prepare his signature dish: Vietnamese snapper fillets, drizzled sexily with kaffir lime-infused sweet sauce and Vietnamese mint. The smell is enticing. Unfortunately, due to hearing loss, the Baron usually announces his signature dish as 'Vietmanese,' no matter how many times his wife, ex-schoolteacher, corrects him.

The snapper is gently steam baking in a low oven while the rest of the crew down a few bevies. The Baron's wife is on her third pinot gris, not a local brand, some Australian swill under fifteen, she'd picked up at Woolies. It's not like she was a total tightwad. She wanted to support the fine blends developing on all sides of their estate, but forty-nine dollars for a Waiheke sav, really?

'You could buy three Aussie blends for less than that, I mean,' she'd tell people. 'Do the math!' The crossover from high school teacher to domestic goddess had left a bit of a residue.

Back in the kitchen, the snapper is now sizzling juicily and a bon vivant atmosphere *en general* prevails. Enter Leila, the Iraqi boating girlfriend, only on water apparently, of Jack, a fading handsome divorcee who'd recently bought a snappy launch, virtually identical to the Baron's, and fancied himself as a ladies' man. Teetering slightly on her rhinestone cork wedges, Leila had set up a bar area and was serving generous shots of ouzo and whiskey to all who could keep up. Edwin, newly sober for a year, is flirting outrageously with the 'barmaid', his modus operandi with the gentler sex, sipping on a glass of fake champers, listening to her sing-song-Iraqi accent, smelling her musky perfume. God he needed a woman in the worst way.

Jack is outside, holding court with the Baron's wife who he had always had a crush on, while Oscar, her son-in-law, a stroppy builder who has an interesting knack of finding a person's Achilles heel and making it burn, sat nursing a beer. The Baron's wife had been a looker in her day and knew how to tell a good story when she got the chance, not an easy feat with these two braggards. She didn't appreciate it when Jack squeezed her ample butt as she reached for her wine bottle. He was always doing things like that. No wonder his 'boatie girlfriend' was so insecure about their 'relationship.'

'Snapper is ready. Come to the table, people!' The Baron enjoyed a strong command, something he'd picked up from his Grammar school days. The guests jostle their way onto the Flintstone outdoor furniture, their mouths watering. The proud host serves each one a succulent fillet and spoons the sweet Asian sauce over perfect mounds of basmati rice. The babble dies down and all are murmuring about the delicious flavours, devouring their servings like hungry children.

'Yeah, ma mate got me some killer scallops the other day,' Oscar announced between mouthfuls, 'I made a mean feed, best seafood I've ever tasted'. Eyes right to the Baron for a response to the obvious food challenge, but he's oblivious, one of the few benefits of his hearing loss. This Achilles jab flew right by him. Oscar leaned back from the table, proud of his accomplishment. He loved a good stir.

'Oh really? What was your recipe?' piped up the Baroness, always keen to try new recipes. Her girlfriends knew she was prone to tearing tasty ones out of *Cuisine* magazines at the dentist, when no one was looking.

'Well I'm not a farking homo!' Oscar snarls, his eyes wicked, nostrils flaring. He's a Taurus, the Baroness remembered. She was also prone to judging people based entirely on knowing their sun sign.

'Hey, I don't take kindly to that kind of reference!' All eyes on Edwin at the other end of the table. He'd taken exception to gay bashing after his wife left him for another woman.

'Yeah, I'm not *gay* like I'd share recipes and shit.' Oscar is on a roll, every other word is gay or homo. Edwin's colour is rising and his demeanor darkens as he finishes his last mouthful of snapper and rises from his seat.

'Thanks for lunch,' he nods with old school respect to the Baron.

'Bye Edwin', everyone choruses as he shakes hands all round.

Oscar has his hand outstretched, but Edwin flips him the bird, kiwi style, two fingers, then turns on his Cuban heel and walks rather stiffly up the path to his shiny black SUV. He'd had the gold hubcaps removed after some 'boy racer' ribbing he got from his mates.

'If ya take the stick outta yer arse, you'd walk better,' Oscar calls after him.

'What'd ya say?' Edwin's hearing was almost as bad as the

Baron's, but he refused to wear hearing aids, even though he had them, thinking it would affect his 'babe pulling,' which wasn't what it used to be.

'I said, if you take the gay stick outta yer arse, ya might walk better.'

The Baroness thought she saw Oscar's Nikes paw the ground and his nostrils were definitely enlarged.

Edwin stops, reddens, turns on his heal and strides back down the path towards his opponent. He rips off his flannel shirt, buttons actually flying.

The group look on in disbelief at what looks like a scene from a David Lynch film. It is on. Edwin's dukes are up, 'Queensbury rules' style.

Oscar rises to the challenge.

'Ya wanna go boy?' Edwin lunges forward and they're on the ground, rolling down the bank, crushing the Baron's favourite hibiscus. Crunch, crash, small bushes lie flattened, flowers bruise under the pummelling bodies.

'Stop them!' screams the Baroness.

'Call 911, call 911,' screams Leila, getting a better view on top of the bench. Drunk on ouzo, she had somehow plugged into the American emergency phone number.

'Please stop them Jack!' The Baroness is beside herself, her freckled hands waving about watching their beautiful garden being destroyed as the two hot heads thrash about.

Edwin has blood trickling down his face and Oscar's shirt is torn, his face is white with adrenalin. Jack watches, mildly amused at the two grown men battling it out, entertaining even. He smiles showing his handsome perfect teeth, one of his more alluring features which usually pulled in the most cagey sheilas, 'No way, I'm not getting in the middle of *that*.'

'Bloody Aquarian,' the Baroness muses, 'self centered prick.'

'911, call 911!' Leila is dangerously close to the edge of the bench, waving her rhinestone iPhone.

'What could have gotten into Edwin? He's being so aggressive!' the Baroness asks her.

'Maybe it was the wheesky?'

'What whisky?'

'Well, I was adding shots of wheesky into his fake champagne, cheer him up.'

'Bet she's a Leo,' the Baroness is not amused, 'or maybe a Cancer.' She gives the Baron a knowing look as another hibiscus plant bites the dust. She's taken back to when she was a shy schoolgirl at primary school, before iPhones, iPads, hell, even before colour TV and the most exciting entertainment was when a fight broke out in the playground, the adrenalin, the smell of sweat and blood, and, her school chums, well behaved polite young ladies, uniforms pressed, first white bras inside crisp white blouses, transfixed in a circle chanting: *fight, fight, fight*. It was sexy, primal even. A *Lord of the Flies* scene in the middle of the pristine Hawkes Bay schoolyard. *Fight, fight, fight!*

Finally, the two battlers come to a standstill with Oscar astride his crumpled opponent, holding back from delivering another blow. He stands up still eyeballing Edwin and adjusts what's left of his shirt.

The old scrapper gets to his feet slowly, looks around the group of drop mouthed onlookers then starts towards his 'babe magnet' car.

'That the best you can do old man?' Oscar couldn't help himself. His mother always said he went too far at times, didn't know when to stop. This was one of those times.

Edwin spins around, dukes up, knees wobbling, shaking the

sweat and blood from his forehead, 'Ya wanna go again boy? Shoulda taken me on when I was younger, *cunt*!' He hisses out the last words almost in disgust, not too impressed with the aging process and all it's alarming side affects.

Even the tuis above, silent during the whole debacle, wait for the response.

Tripping in Melbourne with Mum and the Indian Prince

It all started off well enough and I was quite proud of the job I'd done booking flights, hotels and a rental car. It was Thursday morning and Gary, my mother and I were comfortably checked-in at the Great Western Hotel on Spencer Street. Gary systematically unpacked his bags as I drove Mum to her hair appointment at David Jones on Bourke Street.

'Just a wash and set,' she'd requested back home. 'It will last a week and look nice for the wedding on Saturday.'

It was my first time ever driving in Melbourne. I'd studied the thick city map book in the shiny marble bathroom before leaving. I loaded my shrinking mother, Margaret, into our sporty black Camry rental and proceeded out of the hotel car park and into the stream of city traffic.

'Oh look at that, how funny. Jolimont Pleasure garden, wonder what goes on there?'

Mum was basically pointing out anything and everything that caught her fancy, down the six or so city blocks to David Jones, while I navigated the hectic streets, one way, two-way, tram lines, actual trams.

'Oh, look at that man and his wife. Goodness aren't some of these Australians overweight?'

Ignoring her, I focused intently on the street names as they flashed by, Collins Street, Little Collins Street. They drive fast here. At last at the corner of Elizabeth and Bourke Street, I spied David Jones.

'I can't park outside Mum. It's all tram tracks.' City trams were shunting to and fro. 'I'll pick you up at that corner ok?'

As she slowly descended to the curb, I worried if she'd remember the instructions and ignored the road rage congesting behind me. In the rear view mirror I could see her making a beeline to the entrance of David Jones, her turquoise trouser suit blending and fading into the maze of upwardly mobile Melbournites, crossing at the lights. Silently asking for help that she would be safe, I gunned the Camry back to the hotel.

Later I raced up three floors of David Jones. I had left Gary with the car on an Elizabeth Street loading zone, and had seen no sign of Mum on the corner, any corner. It was thirty-six degrees outside, the hottest October day in Melbourne in a hundred years and I'd lost my eighty-year-old mother.

'Oh, the white-haired lady, she left a while ago,' the false eye lashes at David Jones flicked her hair back as she swished away.

'Where the hell is she?' I shield my eyes from the bright Australian sun and scanned all the street corners again. Had she been kidnapped, mugged? There was no sign of her anywhere.

'She hasn't got the hotel name or number,' back at the car I am panicking.

'Lets go back to the hotel and see if she's there,' Gary says cranking the rental into second gear. We careen down La Trobe Street at full speed. My mobile interrupts at the lights.

'Katy, I have your mother here,' a warm well-spoken Indian man's voice.

"Oh my god, where are you?'

'We are downtown. What is the name of the hotel please?'

Details are exchanged as Gary 'two tyres' round the corner into Spencer Street and I smell rubber.

'There she is!' I'm ecstatic at the sight of her silver white head, now coiffed with feathered curls, at the entrance of the Atlantis Great Western.

'You know,' she later told us with pride, 'he was such a lovely young man. He got out of the taxi three times to try and call your mobile. Then he called his mother in New Zealand to get the country code. You never know your luck in a big city.' She winked like a showgirl, giggled and took a ladylike sip of the Earl Grey tea I'd made her. 'I asked how much the fare was and he said nothing, so I gave him fifty.'

'Jeez that was generous, Mum, but very kind.' I wondered at her judgment, knowing she only had a hundred and fifty dollars spending money for the five-day trip.

'And so handsome,' she smiled, enjoying the memory.

Okay, we've all been swayed by a pretty face, I thought, subtly feeling her forehead and checking vital signs, hoping there'd been no permanent damage from the intense heat of the day. How do you feel for a pulse again? She didn't even have a hat or sunglasses. How could we? I cranked up the air conditioning.

'I think I'll go lie down now, dear.' Okay good, that was normal for her.

I peered into her bedroom later. It was as cool as a tomb and she lay on top of the white doona, perfectly straight, hands folded on her chest like a mummy, my mummy, very still, but oh Jesus. I felt her wrist and then put my palm up to her nose to feel her breath. All good. God I need a drink.

Sleeping in the chilled hotel rooms seemed to suit Mum who appeared refreshed the next morning, as she brightly searched for the Earl Grey. Unfortunately, my reaction was not so positive, and I developed a severe cold with fever, which was a worry because I had to sing at my cousin's wedding in Mornington, the next day. Resorting to evil remedies in this emergency, I procured some over-the-Australian-counter 'flu medicine with an alarming percentage of pseudoephedrine. I discovered this after I'd dropped 2 capsules and was now lost in the maze of the Melbourne art gallery, speed reading every artist's bio. Leaving Gary, with Mum on his arm, way back in European Traditional, I was eyeballing the canvas in the Abstracts.

'Hurry up you slowpokes!' I shouted back at them. They appeared in the distance as abstract shapes: mottled turquoise and shades of grey. *I'm hallucinating on these meds.* 'Wave your hand so I know it's you.'

Gaza's long familiar arm made a black line out from the larger grey shape and I breathed. It was just the drugs.

'Don't be so rude to your mother, darling. She's just trying to keep up.'

'I know but she's so frigging slow. I can't stand it and why are all these other shapes in here taking so long to read the bios? It's doing my head in.' I sniffed into my tissue like a junkie, eyes still spinning following hours of intense abstracting. It was only day two.

'Come on Margaret, yes that's right. It's fifty-seven steps down here. You've been counting, haven't you?'

The Abstract Mode display, at the National Gallery, with fashion and textiles from the nineteenth century to present day and the futuristic 1960's styles of Pierre Cardin were literally blowing my mind, while Mum, slowly and drug-free, adored the contemporary designs by Christian Dior and John Galliano.

Leaving the gallery, Gary and I took her by the arms, much like the way she and Dad had swung me as a child.

'I wonder if I'll see my taxi driver,' Mum said as we drove back to the hotel, scanning the yellow cabs at the many ranks.

On our last day in Melbourne, we pulled into a gas station by the airport to top up the tank of the Camry. I noticed that gas was much cheaper than New Zealand.

'There he is,' Mum was ecstatic. Sure enough there was the handsome Bollywood taxi driver smiling at her from the window of his shiny cab. Mum waved like the Queen Mother and he turned and saluted her in an old worldly manner. Her pale rose complexion blushed and her blue eyes sparkled.

Not bad going for 80, I thought as I went to pay for the gas. What's the likelihood of seeing him again in a city of four million and over forty thousand taxis? On the flight home I considered the possibility that this handsome kind spirited young man had perhaps been a guardian angel for my kind-hearted mother, who must have banked some serious good karma over her eighty years. And that even in this world of chaos and war, there are still honourable, decent people, who know what it's like to be lost in a big city.

No Room for Virgins at the Feminist Bookstore

roudly armed with my new series of Madonna cards, I stepped into that shrine of womanhood on Ponsonby Road. It was a bit of a stretch but I'd been successful at the last card store and this was close to the bus stop. It was 4.00 pm and it was getting cold and I was shooting for the 5.00 pm ferry home. With a warm and confident air, I approached the hipster dyke at the counter with my hand outstretched and introduced myself.

'I've just painted a series of Guadalupe Madonnas and made them into cards,' I told her, remembering not to rush the delivery, *leave some space*. 'She was the symbol carried by the United Farm Workers Union during their protest marches in the Seventies. Remember the grape boycotts in California?'

'Are you selling them?' She peered over her slim black reading glasses, grey-white fringe coiffed, no make-up. She was busy straightening some black and white Pocketbook Penguin editions into a neat pile.

'Yes I am,' I beamed.

'I'm sorry but the owner is busy at the moment,' she said in an undertone, *busy* delivered in a stage whisper.

'I'm happy to leave some samples,' undeterred by the lack luster response. I watched her make a perfect pile of Brave Wonderful Women bookmarks in pure OCD style, her grey eyes darting around the store.

'You can't just *come* in here without an appointment,' boomed the larger than life manager, glaring at me from across the room. She was holding court with a fresh-faced preppy woman, sitting across from her in a large overstuffed armchair.

'Well, I just popped in on the off-chance,' I said in my defence. 'You see I'm over from Waiheke Island for the day.'

'Oh, Waiheke,' the manager beamed up at me, 'well if you want to wait, I'll see you soon.' She waved her chubby hand towards a forlorn Edwardian reclining chair that had seen better days.

'Oh, yes,' Preppy blushed prettily on, 'North and South are doing an article and the Herald's also doing a decent write up...' She was obviously terribly excited about the press for her client's new release, *Babygate Two: Beyond Parenthood and the Workplace*.

Gathering up my precious Madonnas, I made my way to the designated area, armed with *Pictures of Dangerous Women*, for perusing and settled in for a period of waiting. The images were delightful: black and white shots of women from the Thirties; women boozing; women smoking; women smoking and boozing; women smoking and boozing on motorbikes; women boozing and smoking in silky lingerie lounging around on brass beds with other dangerous boozing 'wimen', also smoking. It was a fascinating read. On sale for fifty dollars, I wondered if my husband would like it. He quite liked wild women. Not a very feminist thing to think, I chided myself.

Crossing my legs and settling into the chair, I drew the Guadalupe cards slowly out of my bag and examined them. Six carefully painted Madonnas in bold, lively colours. The Lady of Guadalupe, a powerful symbol of Mexican identity and faith, representing motherhood, feminism and even social justice. I thought of the UFW marches in the seventies, with hundreds of Mexican farmworkers and their families, walking for miles, holding the Madonna for protection, protesting without violence.

They were so brave.

I loved my bold Madonna images and was proud of them, hoping they'd be appreciated. I was startled back to the present, when the manager's voice rang out. 'Thanks for coming in and looking forward to the release!' she farewelled Preppy.

Feeling rather childlike squatting in the low-slung chair, with my long brown leather boots and bright orange coat and scarf, I waited to be summoned.

'I can see you now, I only have five minutes!' The manager raised her bushy eyebrows in my direction. Francis Ford Coppalla should have such eyebrows, I mused, unbending my legs and straightening myself up to full size.

'I made this series of Guadalupe Madonnas.' I was beginning to sound like one of those kids who are selling chocolate bars to raise money for camp. I felt about that age in front of this formidable manager, with her big legs, piercing dark eyes, making me feel lucky to be sitting opposite her, like casting couch syndrome.

'Well I don't know,' she thumbed through my cards with her stubby fingers. 'I see, mmmm, yes, I don't really know.' She took a couple of them over to OCD and they conferred in hushed tones, behind the counter, their backs to me. 'Mmmm,' 'Mmmm,' nodding and fingering the cards thoughtfully. I didn't like the signs.

The manager came back and sat down. The large Edwardian chair sighed as she re-manspread her legs, leaning back with her arms behind her head. The combination of sitting in the low chair and the dismissive reception had rendered me child-like and I felt my sales pitch shriveling like a popped balloon. However I carried on anyway. *Hey, maybe I will get to go to camp!*

'Well, I lived in California in the seventies, during the United Farm Workers' Union Strikes. My Cuban husband was part of the union and we had house meetings in our home in Woodland. Cesar Chavez led them to victory. They carried the Madonna high during the marches. She was a symbol to give them hope!' I felt myself getting excited and remembered to slow down. The word *husband* went down like a dead balloon, as did the mention of Cesar Chavez. There were no signs of anything remotely male in the bookstore.

'No.' she replied emphatically. 'No,' she repeated so loudly that the aged hipster in the self help section stopped reading *Mama Gena's School of Womenly Arts*, and glanced over in our direction.

My cheeks burned as she went on. 'We don't really have anything with religious connotations in here. Thanks for coming in though. Oh, and I love your tights.' She smiled and I think she may have been flirting. 'My friend says it's just gorg on the island today. She's over there.' She watched me as I gathered up my rejected Madonnas.

'Yes Waiheke's lovely,' I managed with a lump in my throat, clumsily putting the cards back in my black shoulder bag.

Win some, lose some, I was thinking as I pushed the heavy door open to the busy street. The cold wind whipped around my shoulders as I crossed the street to the bus stop and I wrapped my warm scarf one more time around my neck and hailed the Link bus.

Fuck you feministas. I thought as the Linky rattled down College Hill Road. I had become a feminist in the sixties and had burned my bras in defiance of the patriachy. I thought of when my daughter Sarah and I marched with thousands of other women up Queen Street in '83. Twenty thousand women joined together, singing and protesting about the American Nuclear ships coming to New Zealand.

The overly full Linky struggled up Victoria Street. I thought about the vision of a translucent Madonna which appeared in my mind during a harmonizing session with my friend Sylvie. The Madonna's beauty and pure grace filled me with love. I remembered weeping. The vision stayed with me for years and was the inspiration for my paintings. Sylvie said the Madonna was my guardian angel. I wasn't a Catholic but I knew that vision was pure, forgiving love.

Yes we need more of that in the world I thought as I walked past a bus stop on way to the ferry. A middle aged homeless woman had set up her base there, with grey woollen blankets and newspapers. I watched her pacing around inside the shelter, then she slid down her grubby track pants, crouched and pissed in the corner, like a dog. Her urine ran like a shiny stream out into Victoria Street where polished cars revved at the lights. Businessmen and women couldn't help but watch her bare brown bottom through the glass. Yes we definitely need more love for humans in this world.

Whoever said cold calling would be easy, I was thinking as I hurried on to the waiting ferry, especially when you're pimping virgin cards in a feminist bookstore.

File This

rs. Brenda O'Sullivan sat slightly sprawled out on the wooden kitchen chair, filing her long manicured nails with a shiny retro file. She glanced over at the wooden bench and noticed some Vogels crumbs left on the breadboard. His crumbs, she thought, his crumbs from his bloody toast. He can bloody well wipe them up himself! A fly buzzed lazily 'round the compost bucket.

His job, she muttered, filing faster, the file slashing the air space like little jets 'round the skyscraper nails. Why does he have to leave it so long before he empties the bloody thing? She whacked the fly dead with one swat of the file and flicked a strand of lank, black hair behind her ear. She looked around her kitchen. She'd been so happy when they'd first bought No 37 Sea View Road. Ecstatic, she'd invited all their friends for a housewarming. Tom had grilled steaks on the barbie and Brenda thought they'd 'arrived.' She had topped up the sauvignons and chatted easily with the neighbourhood women about how full their water tanks were and where they were going for their holidays.

They had belonged here in this comfortable community.

The dining table was worn from the constant wiping, eating, wining, spilling, and the purple irises she'd bought for herself last Thursday at Woolies drooped forlornly in the squat glass vase. The kitchen clock ticked loudly in the silence of her life and she felt like she was waiting for something. What it was she didn't know but she had a creepy feeling it was bad news of some kind. Brenda wrapped her soft dark blue robe around her and slopped into her fluffy slippers and out the back door to the letterbox. The street was quiet, waiting. The Postie's motorbike putted off around the corner. She flicked out the local paper and read the front headlines – Rats: *A Threat to Safety of Island community. Some more discussion about oversized shop signs, businesses outraged!*

'That was all in last week's Marketplace,' she muttered, quietly shushing up the gravel pathway to the bored comfort of her kitchen. A blue envelope spilled out from the folds of the paper and on to the floor where it was almost swallowed by the fuzz of her slipper. She bent down to pick it up, her long hair falling heavily around her face. She recognized the large seductive handwriting.

Attention: Ms. Brenda O'Sullivan
37 Sea View Road
Onetangi
Waiheke Island

Ms, she murmured, rummaging nervously for a cigarette from the depths of her robe. She lit it on the gas burner and used the sharp file to tear open the letter.

Dearest B,
Forgive me for writing but it's been so long since we've
spoken and I need to see you. I've had some terrible news
and I need to talk to you.
I'll explain everything.
Can you meet me at my place? I've moved back to
Ponsonby and my number's changed; 361 5539

It's really important or I wouldn't be asking.

C.

Brenda read the letter over and over trying to get to grips with what it said. She hadn't spoken to her ex, Charles, for over five years. Since their divorce there had been nothing to say. She remembered the sight of him with her best friend, Allison, snuggled up together at Cin Cin's. His long cheating arm drooped around her bare shoulders.

They hadn't noticed her. They'd thought she was at writing class. But she'd been suspicious when she'd heard him on the phone and more so when he'd told her he had a 'biz thing' after work on Wednesday. He wouldn't be long and she had class anyway. Then a few weeks later he told her he'd fallen for someone else and she found out the someone else, was her best friend from high school. The betrayal still ate at her insides and consumed her with a rage she'd not thought possible. She had destroyed all his shirts with a razor and flung them out on the lawn. They lay there, pastel, shapeless ribbons on the dewy morning grass.

He moved out after that and she'd imagined that he and Allison were blissfully happy and that had made her even more angry. She'd call them at 3.00 am after too many savs and yell horrible things down the phone. She swore and screamed and felt really good afterwards. Her girlfriends had told her to stop that, said she'd be arrested.

So eventually she did stop and moved on. Two years later she met Tom on findsomeone.co.nz and they had moved in together.

Now, three years later and two lazy flies were buzzing 'round the compost. Fucking flies! She stabbed one with the nail file and fried it over the gas flame, smiling while it sizzled. The smell of burning fly flesh made her long nose crinkle with distaste. *So, the bastard wants to see me does he?* This will be good, she thought, checking out her reflection in the new stainless steel fridge. She'd wanted it so bad; all the girls were getting them. Nobody had white-wear anymore. It was so passé!

The dark circles under her eyes made her look tired and her hair, which had always been her best feature, had lost its shine. She opened up her robe and her breasts looked long and unloved, her hips fuller, wanting. *What the hell, it might be fun to taunt the old bastard. Wonder what's happened for him to get in touch after all this time? Two fifteen better think about dinner I suppose. Monday night equals Shepherd's Pie.* It was now a routine, imposed over the years by Tom. At first his need for routines and discipline had seemed old fashioned, old worldly, charming, but that too had lost its shine. *I'll leave Tom a note. Make up something. As long as the pie's in the oven and the Steinies are in the fridge, he'll hardly notice I'm gone.*

She picked up the slim line to call her ex. It had been so long since she'd heard his voice, she was startled by her own response.

'Brenda, is that you?' His deep voice still got her going.

'Yes what's the matter?' It sounded urgent.

'Can you come over?'

'I suppose so. Where are you?'

'I'm on Blake Street, Apartment 15, at number 10. I really need to see you Brennie.'

'Okay, I'll get the 5.00 pm ferry tonight. See you then'.

She nestled the stainless steel slim line back into its cradle and started on the pie, peeling the spuds in quick jerky motions. *Damn this bloody designer peeler. It's hopeless!* She almost cut her thumb.

After a long hot shower, her black hair towel dried and smelling like lavender, she chose her black genuine leather skirt for the rendezvous, fishnet stockings and her new black cowboy boots. She tossed her deep red velvet scarf around her slim neck and liked what she saw in the hall mirror. Opera red on her lips, that should get him going. She winked at her reflection.

Her note on shopping list paper, propped up limply against the vase, read:

Dear Tom,
Had to go into Smith & Caughey's to take that blue
woollen skirt back, (the one you said made my bottom
look fat).
Will grab some tea at Jenny's and have a catch up.
Back on late ferry.
B. XX
PS. Monday pie in oven.

The Link bus pulled into the bus stop outside 'Rare Books' and Brenda stepped off lightly on to the familiar worn footpath. Ponsonby househusbands sipped lattes, rocking their organically fed, round faced babes in mountain strollers, and swapped recipes.

Things have changed, Brenda mused as she strode across the pedestrian crossing. Five years had seen changes to their old stomping ground. 'Java Jive' was gone and designer clothes stores stood where the old Gluepot used to be. God that night they saw Koko Taylor upstairs at the Gluepot, changing, everything changing. Her black boots clicked determinedly passed the old entrance to Java Jive, now a smart real estate office. They'd had so many good nights down there, her and Charles. Yes, Charlie boy was a lot of fun when he wanted to be.

Charles opened the door of his single mans' apartment. He gave Brenda a look over, admiring her. 'Great to see you, Babe! You look way sexy in that skirt.'

Just the same ol' Charlie, she thought, with his dark good looks and predictable come on. A cold bottle of sauvignon, under fifteen dollars, and two glasses waited for her on the card table.

Charles slung into the nearest folding chair and opened a packet of Dunhills.

Brenda slowly draped her leather jacket over the other chair and sat down, accepting a cold glass and a cig from Charles. She looked round at what had become of his world and smirked. To think he'd end up in some bleak bed-sit. Not really up to scratch for ol' styley Charlie. He leaned over and lit her cigarette seductively, cupping his long fingers to protect the flame.

Old flame, she thought quietly, my old flame. She blew smoke above his head and looked him in the eyes.

'Okay, so what's the big important news?'

'Yeah, right. Well, Ally kicked me out.'

'Really, when did that happen?'

'Last month. She kept all the furniture, everything. I only got the old waterbed after a fight through my lawyer.'

Brenda gazed over at the colourful, 70's, patch-worked classic and couldn't help remembering some good times there also. 'You can take the boy outa Henderson...' she was thinking. She was gloating, laughing to herself, but she kept her cool, even enjoyed his despair, serves him right. At the same time she couldn't help but remember how great he was in bed.

'What happened?'

He chuckled darkly, 'Oh, you know, she caught me in bed with someone.'

'Really? Who?'

'You wouldn't know her, someone from work, a young chick, really hot actually.'

'So, that's your news?' Brenda gulped some wine down.

Yeah, well I'm pretty gutted, haven't been able to sleep for days'.

'Really?'

Brenda remembered his shirts, lifeless and bland on the lawn and noticed how his style had changed, trendier these days, less conservative, striped shady autumn tones, showing off his tan. She crossed her long brown Nudie-Beach-legs and sipped her chilled Sav slowly taking him in. *What was next?*

'Yeah, well how's things going with what's his name?' Charles dragged sexily on his Dunhill.

'Tom?'

'Yeah, Tom.' Smoke filled up the space between them.

'Oh, great, you know. We're all settled over on the island. It's great.' Brenda could hear her tone, lifeless, flat, bored mentioning her new life.

'Oh, really? Oh, too bad. I was rather hoping it had all turned to shit by now. You know, used by date and all that, thought we could give it another round maybe?'

'Really you did, eh?'

'C'mon, Brennie. You know we're good together. I miss that, miss you.' He was pleading, those eyes.

'Just roll back into bed, eh, like old times. That's what you thought ol' Charlie boy?'

'Yes, actually, I was rather hoping.' He smiled sheepishly, like a little boy now.

Brenda took a long sip of the cold white and looked him over. Her fingers clasped the cheap wine glass so hard she thought it might crack. 'Got any dak?' She smiled, enjoying her position, on top of his game.

Charles nodded and pulled a worn kauri tobacco tin from his jacket pocket. 'This is some primo outdoors bud,' he confided proudly, 'from up north, Hokianga.'

Brenda watched his familiar long brown fingers roll up the sticky bud and all the things she'd always liked about him came rushing back, his musky scent, 'White Musk Cologne,' his suave style, his swagger, like a rock star'. *No, don't go there. Don't get sucked in. He's a bastard remember? A cheat, a slut of a man.* But the sweet strong bud did its magic and she felt her body responding to his light touch as he stroked her face and talked his talk, the familiar voice, the tone, rich and soft in her ear. She felt his hands running over her boots, up inside her fishnet thighs. She was gone. He had her.

The ride on the waterbed was all too familiar, the roll and sway, like gentle waves and Charlie, naked tanned and strong above her, his eyes closed and smiling. She'd actually forgotten how good he really was, how handsome and how beautiful his creamy skin felt.

'Oh God, Ally, Ally, Oh God!' He cried out like he was dying and fell back against the waves.

After, Brenda felt the old rage, fury, bubbling through her veins like hot steam, watching him lying there, crashed out. She couldn't believe she'd let him in after all this time, the fucking bastard!

On the ferry back home she remembered how quickly she'd reached for the file. His expression she'd never forget. His beautiful sleepy face harshly awakened. 'No Brennie, No!' His flat brown eyes pleading, the blood, crimson water bubbling up. She'd never forget.

Brenda threw it overboard after she'd tidied herself in the loo. Damn file, it was too sharp anyway. She made a mental note. 'I'll get an emery board in Oneroa on Thursday, and a Gulf News.' She powdered her long nose in the compact mirror and noticed for the first time the dark love bite blooming, a crimson rose, on her slender neck. Damn, how am I going to explain that? She wrapped her long red scarf one more time round her neck and prepared to disembark.

Made in Germany

here she was again, tottering on cork wedgy slip-ons, her black faux-fur jacket tossed like a nightclub singer's to the floor by the ATM. The blue mumu hung limply off her swampy shoulders and she gazed at me quizzically, not recognizing me in her valium haze. Her expression as she tries to focus would be comical if she wasn't in her late eighties. I knew she didn't remember my visit, didn't remember me at all. Had she forgotten her password? Did she think I knew it?

The garage sale was where I first encountered this faux-fur nana, advertised in the Gulf News as a, 'Not to be missed. Furniture, beds, table and knick knacks.' I wove carefully round the bends on Wilma Road and parked across from the modern bach, set back from the road. No car. The porch door was open. I peeked in.

'Anyone home?'

'Just a minute, I'll get some clothes on.' A high-pitched, muffled voice from inside.

I waited in the cloistered hallway for a few minutes then entered slowly into the smoky haze of her living room. She stood there, naked with her back to me, struggling with her muumuu. The old gas heater was fuming and cranked up high.

'Too hot, can't stand clothes in this heat.' Her high-pitched cackle was disturbing.

With a quick perusal of the bargains I decided most items

were overpriced and it looked like she was either packing to go away or unpacking after a trip.

'Are you moving?' I inquired politely.

'No', she cackled, 'I'm just getting a new bedroom set.'

That didn't explain the piles of belongings everywhere, like they were waiting to be plumped into a cardboard box.

'Two hundred and fifty bucks for the dinette set.' Her voice was like a raspy sheep.

I gave the tasteless smoky glassed table and chipped chairs the once over. 'No thanks.' A collection of Mexican vases and pottery took my eye. 'How much for the vase?' It was round with stripes around the neck. I liked the blood red oval blobs.

'Eight bucks.' She'd managed to pull her grey-blue mumu down over her sagging flesh. No undies.

I pulled out a twenty. 'Do you have change?'

'No sorry honey, gave all my change to that damn taxi. Cost me twenty-five bucks from Woolies. Robbers they are, robbers!'

I was still holding the vase.

'See if there's something else you like.' She grinned.

Now I wanted the vase but I also wanted to get out of that motel-like humid room, in constant flux, impermanent, the kitchen unused and sterile. I turned the clay vase over in my hand and noticed it was made in Germany. So not authentically Mexican, faux Mexican, eh? Underneath scratched into the clay, *To Pricilla, with love always, Stefan. X 1943*. Who was Stefan, and was this blue vision of motel wreckage, Pricilla? 'Well I could take this pottery jug and these little brass bowls?'

'Twenty bucks for the lot.' She snaffled my paper money with all the speed of a K Road hooker and shoved it deep in her black faux leather bag. She dug out a pack of Holiday cigarettes, lit one and nestled back down on the 'For Sale' sofa.

'Two hundred and fifty bucks.' She patted it affectionately, dropping ashes all over the worn arm.

Ya gotta be joking, I thought. The threads were hanging forlornly and the checkered cover was so worn that the black had faded to grey and the white squares were also grey. It was more like a worn grey sofa.

"Who's Stefan?" I said almost to myself.

"Ya wanta drink?"

I checked my watch, 10.35 am.

She swung round to the cardboard box wedged between the sofa and the greasy foot spa and pulled out a bottle of Jacobs Creek Merlot.

"Get me some glasses, honey."

Her voice grew softer as she drank the red wine, the glass wobbling in her bony grasp. She sipped and closed her eyes, rocking slightly. Her chipped fingernails tapped on the glass and she started humming, *'Bei Mir Bistu Shein, Bei Mir Bistu Shein, Bedeutet, Du bist der Schönste im ganzen Land...'* She looked over at me with her eyes half closed. 'He's coming soon. I'm all packed and ready. He's bringing me a diamond ring from his Mother in Munich. We're getting engaged and we're getting married after the war.' She smiled to herself and her eyelids slowly opened. One tear rolled down her sagging cheek. She held out her glass for more merlot. 'Stefan, yes. We met in Munich in 1943. Ooh, you wait till you meet him, he's so handsome, so clever and sooo romantic.'

She pulled her mumu out from under her and smoothed down the hem, remembering. 'And so brave to stand up to the Nazis like that, and him being German. I'm so proud of him. He's my hero. They were organizing against the Gestapo. Stefan had been in the Hitler Youth when he was a boy. Saw the Jewish women digging trenches and stuff, knew they were all heading for the death chambers.' Pricilla took a long swig and went on. 'He joined "The White Rose," when he went to Uni. That's where we met. I was a war correspondent in Munich in those days, just out from New Zealand.

The Resistance started there. It was non violent. They put out pamphlets about the what those Nazi buggers were really up to, killing off weak and mental Germans and all the Jews of course. Hitler said they would weaken the bloodline. The Aryan Super race had to be pure. Bah, Hitler what an animal!'

She coughed harshly into her hand. 'They'd probably put me down, now.' She laughed out loud. 'Stefan told me how they would paint a cross over the swastika and paint slogans like "Hitler the Murderer," "Down with Hitler,"' she cackled and her eyes filled with watery tears. 'They were so brave. Stefan was so brave. Top me up would you dear, all this talking's making me thirsty.' She took a long drag on the diminishing ciggie and held out her glass. Her hand had stopped shaking and there was a pale rose blushing in her cheeks.

'Where is Stefan taking you?' I asked.

'On our honeymoon silly.' She winked slyly, and, in the light filtering through the yellowed Venetians, her face looked softer, younger. With the help of the wine, I could just see wartime Pricilla, in love, alive.

She went on remembering, almost to herself. 'I still can't tell Daddy. It's got to be a secret, just like the movement. We've got to elope, go to London. Stefan has friends there. We'll be able to be together forever. Daddy hates the Germans. *Gerries* he calls them. Even though I've told him Stefan's in the resistance, he's still another *bloody Gerry* as far as father's concerned. Is there any more wine left, dear?' She asked with a sly smile, 'Never mind. I'll get us another one.'

The screw-on-top came off faster than a Nazi bullet and Pricilla splashed more red into our glasses and continued. 'Do you wanta see a picture of Stefan dear?' She smiled and was in sepia tone now and grainy.

I must make this my last glass. I looked at my watch it was 11.30. *Where did that hour go?*

'Hand me that box on top of the sideboard would you please?'

The shoebox was an Italian brand, Capriccio, 1950's, black and rust. Pricilla gulped some more merlot and began rustling through the dog-eared prints, and pamphlets, her glass tipping dangerously. 'Here we are in Munich,' she cried out when she found the worn Box Brownie snapshot taken in front of a big school or church. 'There, that's us at the University, that's where we met.'

A handsome square jawed man in white shirt, suit jacket and dark slacks, holding hands with a real beauty. The old black and white print now faded into a pinkish grey. There was young Pricilla with a blonde pageboy cut, perfectly smooth, mohair sweater and a dark tailored skirt, the shoes, high black Italian numbers with ankle straps. Even with the sepia photograph there was no mistaking Pricilla's adoration for this young man. Her Garbo-like profile tilted up towards him, smiling shyly. Stefan clasps her hand proudly and stands tall like a soldier, eyes forward, beaming.

'We'd just spent the night together. He held me all night, said he'd love me forever.' Her face was glowing now with the memory, shining.

An aged pamphlet fell from the pile of memorabilia, written in the uneven ink of an old typewriter. It was in German but English translation was penned in a spidery cursive beneath it:

The German people slumber on in their dull, stupid sleep and encourage these fascist criminals... Who among us has any conception of the dimensions of shame that will befall our children and us, when one day the veil has fallen from our eyes and the most horrible crimes.... reach the light of day?

I wanted to read more but my hostess was on a roll. 'Let's have some music!' Pricilla's faded blues were sparkling now. She got up and went to another box, pulling out an old LP and struggling a bit to steady herself, clicked the arm down and the needle hit the vinyl. *Baby won't you please come home, your Mama miss ya, Daddy won't ya please come home,* crackled out through the vintage hi-fi.

Pricilla held out her arm and grasped mine, "Come on, have a dance," she cackled and swung her hips suggestively, the old dress swirled in the cramped space.

I put down my half empty glass and politely deferred the offer, afraid of dancing even more into her flashback. I could already see the big dancehall, the big band all in white uniform and the silk skirts twirling.

Pricilla was away in her daydream, singing quietly to herself and swaying on the spot to the next song. *Stormy weather, since my man an I ain't together, keeps on raining all the time.*

I closed the porch door quietly. The rain was spitting down on the tin roof and grew heavy as I ran out to the car, the vase and bowls rattling inside my jacket pockets.

'Hey you!'

A man approached in an oilskin and gumboots. Waving at me he walked over to my door.

I lowered the window but not too far, the rain was pelting down.

'How's the old girl today?' He had a weathered face, inside the hood of his coat, and was probably in his early sixties. Rain was making rivulets down the oilskin, splashing on to the window.

'Oh, Pricilla? She seems quite happy right now.'

'Yeah, well it's a damn shame. I keep an eye on her. Damn shame what happened to her fiancé. She never got over it. Can I get in the car? This rain's pissing down out here.'

Oh boy, what a Saturday this was shaping up to be: a naked old drunken lady wanting to get me drunk and dance with her and now this possible serial rapist/killer trying to get in my car. But I did want to know Pricilla's story and I supposed that I could always knock him over the head with Stefan's vase. I gripped it hard in my pocket as Mr. Oilskin slithered into the front seat, taking my stiff silence as an Okay.

'Oooah, that's better.' He slammed the heavy door shut. 'Nice interior. Real leather is it? Dave's the name, Dave Dean!" He extended his large dripping hand and we shook, water spraying all over the *leather* dash. He pulled a battered flask from his pocket and took a long swig. 'Want some?'

I shook my head primly. God, were they all heavy drinkers down this street? I needed a double espresso, not whiskey. I still had to drive home. *But who was I kidding?* Pricilla's warm red wine had done its thing so I took a tiny sip.

'Yeah, well like I say, I know quite a bit about our friend Pricilla. She really should be put away. She's away with the fairies most of the time. Still thinks she's back in World War Two.' The rain was coming down in waves, crashing over the bonnet. Dave's deep voice got louder. 'Well, she met up with this German chappie over in Europe. He was in the Resistance. The White Rose I think it was, yeah that's it. The Gestapo had them all beheaded. Pricilla went crazy. Damn shame.' He took another long swig. 'After that she went on the drink. Lost her war correspondent job, became a Call Girl. She was quite a looker back then,' he smiled with his sharp yellow teeth. 'Started in the Dance Halls and ended up working the streets of London in the end.'

'That's pretty sad. How did she end up on the island?'

'She showed up here in the Eighties.' He coughed and wound down the window to spit. 'Her family had this land as a holiday place, came here to camp for the holidays. When her dad died he left it to her. She had this place built and has been waiting for her man to come back. She's been the holy terror of the street ever since,' he chuckled. 'We all look out for her when she goes off. I've brought her back many times, bags all packed and that bloody fur coat. She's off to meet Stefan from the train. You know there's no train on Waiheke.' Dave laughed again and cleared his throat. 'She stumbles down this gravel road in her best shoes and she can hardly stand up. It's all pretty tragic. She'll have to go somewhere they can keep an eye on her soon. She hitch-hikes, ya know, to the Liquor Barn when she runs outa booze.'

I nodded and was overcome suddenly with an overwhelming sadness and sense of loss, the loss of old Pricilla's love, a love strong enough to be still driving her sixty years later, still as real to her as when they'd first been together, two young people, who'd found a solid true love. That love had been a haven in all that horror and chaos of World War II, and the senseless death of young people, brave enough to stand up to the Gestapo. Then there was the biggest loss of all, all those millions of lives lost in the death camps. I felt cold and shivered.

Dave the 'possible serial killer' sat quietly, the rain pelting down like shrapnel on the German car roof. 'So what did ya buy at the sale?' He leaned in a bit too close to see and I could smell the whiskey, sweet and strong. I gripped the vase harder.

'Nothing really, it was a bit overpriced for what it was.' I lied and drew back from his heavy man presence.

'Well, I'd better be getting home. The wife'll be wondering where I've scarpered off to.' He patted my knee and winked as he opened the door. 'You take care driving in this rain.'

I watched him splosh up the gravel road, the rain bouncing off the oilskin like slippery ball bearings. Why did he volunteer all that, I couldn't help but wonder. But who was I to judge him, or the old girl really? Maybe I'll end up old and naked some day, drunk and confused in a motel, struggling to dress myself. I'd always hoped for a more romantic ending, a terminal illness like Katherine Mansfield perhaps, or, entangled in a silk scarf in a sports car like Isadora Duncan? Not hitchhiking drunk in my housedress and fake fur like Pricilla, with her pale bony thumb out and that glazed expression, not caring if she was some island hoon's next road kill.

He'll be here soon, Stefan, you can meet him. No flirtin' though he's all mine... forever. I understood now why she didn't care if she lived and why she drank to remember a time when she was really loved. I drove carefully, round the ponga laden bends looking forward to the warmth of the fire I knew would be lit, and the warm arms of my love.

Glenda's Lot

SALUTE THE SOLDIER
BACK THE ATTACK
Victory Loan

SALUTE THE SOLDIER
BACK THE ATTACK
Victory Loan

HE'S COMING SOUTH
It's fight
work or perish

ENLIST TODAY

there's a MAN'S
job to be done
VOLUNTEER FOR OVERSEAS SERVICE!

lenda looked up towards the village. Fog was settling in around the streetlamps. She pulled up the woollen collar of her blue tartan coat and buried her face in it. A storm was coming down from the North. She wanted to be home, stoking up the fire and getting out of her work clothes. Her feet hurt. *When's the bloody bus coming? Dolly will be wanting her dinner. She'll be getting mad.* Glenda checked in the Woolies bag. Yes, she'd remembered Dolly's Woman's Day and her soy milk, extra calcium. *Thank God. It didn't do to upset Dolly with a storm coming.*

She pulled on her gloves and gathered up her shopping bags. The island bus, loaded with commuters, heaved into the Oneroa bus stop. Glenda waited for the others, the high school boy with acne and saggy trousers, followed by the damp smelling labourer, with a thermos and hardhat. *Men smelt.*

She took out her lavender scented hankie and pressed it to her cold nose, climbing the bus steps slowly. The dark pulled in around her like a familiar rug and she sat up on the front seat, watching the driver. This was the nice one, always greeted her with a smile.

'How's it going luv? Careful up them steps'

'Here's your stop now, take 'er easy, eh.'

The damp foggy cold hit her as she walked up her gravel road. TV lights blinked behind drawn blinds, families doing familiar things. She smelled a roast chicken dinner being served.

Unlocking the front door, it started: 'What took you so long? I'm starving. Where's my tea? I've been here all day long with no one to talk to, no one to look after me, all day alone and cold. You know I can't keep up that bloody fire!'

Glenda knelt before the old pot belly stove and soon had it roaring. 'Sorry Dolly, the bus was later than usual, some hold up with the ferry probably.'

'Can you make my tea please. I'm starving. Hey move out of the way. I'm trying to watch the news.'

Glenda's shoulders sank and she looked down.

'I'm sorry, Glenny. I just get so lonely and miserable all day alone here and my leg needs to be cleaned again. It's scratching, must be some crumbs or something there. Could you look for me? Ouch, see right in there.'

Glenda knelt at her sister's side and eased out the prosthetic. It had never fitted right and constantly gave Dolly grief. She gently blew the crumbs out.

'That's better. Thank you. I'll be nicer after dins. I promise sister dear.'

Glenda went into the kitchen, a dark rimu-panelled fifties style room with a dinette in sparkled lemon and faded lace curtains over a small sink. She turned on the light, folded her coat over the chrome chair and took off her shoes. She flicked out the calico apron and set to work, turning on the gas burner and filling up the saucepan, humming a tune at just the level her sister couldn't hear: *Runaway my little runaway... a run run run run runaway* It stopped the sound of Dolly's constant tirade and kept Glenda safe as she prepared the evening meal. The pot was soon boiling with peeled spuds and the Signature Range fish cakes were browning under the grill.

Dolly's tirade was just at a low roar over the spuds.

'Bloody John Key! He's made all these promises and now he's changing his tune! Where are the tax breaks? Bring back Muldoon, I say! We knew what we had with ol' Robbie.'

The six o'clock news blazed static life into the tiny cottage, filling up its lonely corners with tales of recession and disaster: *No jobs for qualified uni students... mother arrested for death of two year old...* Only the ads brought some relief.

Glenda hummed in the narrow kitchen, mashing the potatoes fiercely and dolloping them into sloppy hills on the worn china plates. The fish cakes were sizzling as she sprinkled them with chopped parsley. She placed her sister's meal on her favourite TV tray, the one with Princess Di's smiling face-fading now from countless scrubbings- and carried it over to the wheelchair, with small purposeful steps.

'What, fish cakes again! Is it Friday already?'

'Here's your Woman's Day, Dolly.'

'Okay, okay, I can see that. Now let me watch the rest of the news. *Some* people care about what's happening in the world.'

Glenda settled into her favourite spot in the dinette and poured herself a healthy sized brandy, for medicinal purposes. Sitting alone, she looking out the window at the dim lights of the houses across the street, the outside world. Rivulets of condensation were running along the louvres, going in all directions. *Trying to escape, like me, there has to be something better than this life, something better than this. Is this my lot? Is this as good as my lot gets?* This was the mantra Glenda usually went over at this time of night, right before *Close Up*, right after she'd served dinner and before Dolly's meds. She liked how the brandy warmed her mouth and smoothed the edges of her nightly routine. Her fingers felt in the pocket of the apron for the letter. She fingered it, unfolding it slowly, touching the handwriting and whispering his words: *'I'll wait for you at the Britomart, by the escalator, Sunday at noon. I look forward to meeting you. Don't be late, regards Godfrey.'*

"I'm coming Dolly. Yes, I know, two sugars, I know soymilk. No, sorry, I wasn't listening. What did you say?'

The bells from St Peter's church woke Glenda from her dreams. *She was running down a green silky hillside. Her legs were young and brown and the dew from the grass splashed up under her petticoats. She was laughing and her pretty sister Dolly was chasing her, almost catching up.* Then the bells rang, then she woke.

Glenda felt for her glasses on the side table and her slippers by the single bed. Her leather suitcase, packed and repacked many times during the night, waited hopefully at the bedroom door.

'Aren't you awake yet?' It had begun already, the monotone from her sister Dolly, coming from the front room. 'Get me a cuppa. I've been up for ages. Come on lazy bones! Glenda, Glendaaaaahhhhh!'

Glenda hummed as she pulled on her stockings, running her thumb inside, for snags. *I think I'll put my hair up and pop some lippie on, not too bold though.* She caught herself pouting a little in the mirror and fastened a pearl shell clasp in her blonde hair. *Who says it couldn't happen? Arranged marriages happen all the time, they have lower divorce rates don't they?*

She'd noticed Godfrey's ad in the Herald personals a while ago. *'Widower, 60's, short with tidy habits, seeks mature housekeeper for relationship and possible marriage.'* Next came the letter of introduction:

Glenda hummed; 'It's a beautiful day,' as she splashed a large shot of medicinal Brandy into her sister's coffee and stirred in the two sugars longer than usual.

'Here you are Dolly. I'm off to church,' she purred.

'Church, what use is church? Sinners, we're all sinners they tell me. Why do I have to go there to be told that? Go to your so-called church, sister and don't bother to say a prayer for me. I'm already dammed. Look at me. Don't leave me alone. Please, I get so lonely.'

Glenda snipped the cottage door quietly and tied the pale silk scarf to keep her French roll from blowing in the north wind. The storm had been and gone on the island, but there was still a sharp Northerly blowing. She clasped her small suitcase and walked without looking back.

'Church,' Dolly was addressing the TV, 'what use is church? Does it get you to walk again?'

Glenda walked with quick steps and gradually the monotone disappeared. She skipped a couple of slow skips down the gravel road to the bus stop.

Britomart Station, at precisely 12.00 noon, Godfrey, in a tight-fitting grey pinstriped suit, was holding up a homemade sign: GLENDA in squat capitals, black felt on brown cardboard, no frills. He checked his watch again. This was not a good sign, three minutes late. They'd miss the train. *He* was always on time. *There's no excuse for tardiness.* He made a mental cross in Glenda's punctuality column. His short arms were getting tired from holding up the sign. *This is the last bloody time I'm doing this, the last time. Not one woman's measured up to scratch and this one's starting out on the wrong foot, four minutes damn!*

Glenda saw her name as she came down the escalator. She shook Godfrey's damp puffy hand. She noticed his eyes narrow and take stock of her from head to toe then back to head. He smiled showing small tight teeth.

'Good to meet you, finally,' he pumped her slim hand and reached for her suitcase.

'It's alright, I'll take it, thanks,' she smiled prettily, her hand coming back to life.

Good teeth, Godfrey ticked that in the health column but added a cross in the subservient box.

'As you like. We best be getting to Platform Three, Southbound train's due to leave any minute!' He checked his watch again and coughed a dry cough.

Glenda out-strode Godfrey's short legs and reached the carriage ahead of him. He panted behind like a middle-aged badger, wiping beads of sweat from his furry brow.

'I've got your ticket, just get a seat, no, not there, somewhere away from the door and those darkies,' he whispered loudly.

The Samoan students watched him awkwardly making his way down the aisle and sniggered behind their books.

Glenda untied her scarf and folded her coat over her knees. Godfrey bustled into his seat and put his briefcase on his lap. He unsnapped the worn black leather, pulled out a legal pad, coughed and straightened his tie, pale striped polyester with lots of wear left.

Glenda glanced over at the red underlinings and exclamation marks then looked out the window. *State houses flashed by, then graffitied fences, more houses, clotheslines...*

'Thought we might as well get started with the job description', Godfrey coughed, 'responsibilities, duties and whatnot. No need to waste time with chit chat eh?'

Glenda noticed he'd blushed and was blooming like a bright rose on both cheeks. 'Hem,' he cleared his throat and loosened the tie. 'Housekeeper's Daily Schedule,' he read out, 'Six thirty AM, rise to make breakfast. Sister has her meds at six thirty-five AM, refer to clear file, attached. Oh, yes, did I mention my sister? She lives with me. She's an invalid.' He went on, 'Make porridge, toast and tea. G takes five slices and sister takes two. Spread the marg thinly. We're on a tight food budget. G likes plenty of brown sugar and cream on porridge. Sister, Marion, takes non-fat milk, no sugar.

More clotheslines, faded sheets flapping soggily outside chipped weatherboard state houses. A small brown dog yapped at the train, straining at his worn rope tied to a battered corrugated iron fence. Glenda brought out her hankie and sniffed the lavender.

Godfrey droned on. 'Eight O'clock, vacuum all through the house, wipe all baseboards with vinegar and hot water. Nine O'clock, laundry as required. Sister's bed is to be changed daily, due to spillage and accidents.' He coughed. The roses had now fully blossomed.

Factories puffing grey smoke, graffitied fences... Glenda was drifting back, lulled by the rhythm of the train and the familiar droning tone. *The dark mossy tunnel, Dolly falling down, her petticoats ripped and muddy, Glenda trying to hold on to her arm, trying to pull her out, Dolly wet and too heavy and falling further, then disappearing. Finding her, the ambulance, Dolly's young legs, crushed and useless. I should've held on, if only I'd held on...*

Godfrey coughed, reality kicked in. 'Ten o'clock, morning tea, water biscuits only for sister. Assorted biscuits in Aulsebrooks tin, for Godfrey only. Eleven o'clock prepare lunch, (see food allergy lists, attached.)'

Glenda heard his voice droning on. She tuned out and watched the stops as they came into view, Newmarket, Ellerslie, Papatoetoe, watching people stepping on and off, each with their own lives, places to go, sweethearts to kiss, one young man holding a bunch of spring flowers. *Where's my lover? She scanned the faces outside the window. No 'Mr. True Love' on this platform. Nobody seemed to notice her at all. She seemed invisible. Is that what getting old does, rub you out of the picture?*

Godfrey went on, 'Twelve-thirty, go to market to get fresh veggies for dinner, wash all vegetables thoroughly. You can't be too careful in South Auckland,' he added with a furtive look at the nearest 'darkie,' a student who was now giving him the evils.

Short, boring and racist, three crosses in Glenda's mental copybook. Three strikes and you're out Mister!'

'Excuse me,' she said quietly. Glenda rose up from her seat and squeezed past Godfrey's workstation. He had the red highlighter poised over the pad and was making adjustments. Hugely busy, he didn't look up.

The train slowed down at Manurewa and Glenda waited for the doors to open. She alighted quickly on to the platform without looking back. She heard the train pick up speed as she untied her scarf and walked briskly towards the main street. She sensed a new freedom, a new delicious freedom and skipped for a few steps along the concrete path. The sun had come out and warmed her face. She was smiling as she let her long hair shake loose and she breathed out slowly.

She remembered when she'd last felt this alive: *Dancing in the dusky ballroom, her crystal blue tulle gown twirling, honey blonde hair flying, nestled in the arms of her true love, handsome in Navy whites. She could feel his breath on her cheek as they turned and twirled, turned and twirled.* 'A real beauty,' they'd said, before Daniel went away to war, before Dolly's fall and then he didn't come home.'

Glenda walked over the Manurewa Bridge swinging the little suitcase, humming; *'Lover man, oh where can you be?'*

Be My Baby

t was the shame. It wouldn't wash off, even in the shower, no matter how much she scrubbed. It was always there like a slimy film that would never go away. Her life had been great up until *it* all started. Josie clearly remembers waking up at 5.30 am on the morning of her fifth birthday. She remembers the rush of being five and finally going to school. She could hardly wait to get there and learn.

There was something at the end of her bed, an envelope with a card inside, with a 5 on it, a plastic '5' broach, red and bold. Josie pinned it on her starched tartan pinafore, fixed the clasps of her leather brogues and neatly folded the tops of her white school socks. She was all ready for school and she was now officially five. It was all so exciting but no one in the house was up and the excitement inside her could not be confined to the walls of the long claustrophobic hallway with it's narrow brown carpet squares and beige wallpaper.

Josie reached up and grasped the chrome door handle and was soon skipping free, down the sixty three steps to the letter box. She could already count them. She waited for the milk truck, and there it was, a sturdy Bedford lumbering around the corner and Mr. Wallace waving at her warmly, his purplish fingertips exposed through the holes in his grey woollen gloves. His breath puffed out in small clouds before him like a friendly dragon, rattling into view.

She clambered up on the step behind the truck and clasped the frosty bottle carrier firmly, running up and shoving the milk into all the neighbours' letterboxes. Running felt good and it warmed her bare legs, mottled from the cold. The sun, just coming up over Te Mata Peak, bounced off her brown hair bringing out the copper lights. Her deep blue eyes smiled out above her freckled cheeks. She loved helping the milkman. Finally the old grey truck completed the crescent and stopped at Josie's driveway. Mr. Wallace handed her the family's milk carrier.

'Five homogenized and half a pint of cream for you young lady. Thanks for the help,' he said kindly.

'Mum doesn't usually get cream. It's too dear. Must be for my birthday tea. I'm five today, see my broach, five!'

Mr. Wallace chuckled and started up the Bedford. 'Happy birthday, little lady. Have a good first day at school.'

Josie hurried back up the steps, hoping her favourite sister Maeve was awake.

Old sleepyhead, Josie thought. *Wonder what Mum's making me for tea? She usually does my favourite: roast chicken and baked veges, wonder what's for pudding, Pavlova?*

School was good for Josie. She learned to read quickly and soon escalated to Primer Four. She skipped two classes. Mum was very proud, being an Auckland Grammar girl herself, she always talked about the value of a 'Good Education.' That's when *it* started, when she could read well. *They* would come and stay or her family would all drive north to Auckland in her Dad's Hillman Hunter. She remembered the long windy roads to Taupo for morning tea, then Auckland by dinnertime. Maeve would always get carsick and throw up out the window. She was made to wash the 'sick' off the car door when they arrived at their grandparents' house. *It* would always happen then, in the school holidays.

'Here, read this,' Poppa's morning breath whispered secretively in Josie's ear.

She was tucked up in bed next to her grandfather. Maeve was chattering away noisily next to Nana in the other single bed.

Josie studied the text of the book he held, it was wrapped in brown paper. 'Lady Chatterley's Lover', by D H Lawrence she read.

She felt his leathery fingers searching around inside her shortie pajamas, then he touched her. She felt a strange sensation and tried to focus on the story. Why was he showing her this? It was rude. And what was he doing?

Then *it* was whenever he could get her alone, the garage, perhaps, with some fake request for help and he would try again to touch her there. 'Don't say anything, our secret eh?' Then came the presents and the long walks to get fresh bread from the Bread Factory after dinner. 'No Maeve, you stay and help Nana clear the table, Josie will come with me.' The smell of fresh baked bread filled the chilly night air as he forced her small hand into his pocket and made her feel him through the soft cloth of the trouser pocket.

Josie was ten when she learned about sex from the girls at school. They all discussed it at playtime under the shade of the big kauris in the dell. Only her friend Justine didn't know if boys had periods but thought they probably did. Josie wondered where the blood would come from and if they wore special pads, different from girls.

They all knew they would be getting bras soon and Justine had already started her period and was 'quite developed' for her age. She was the first to start wearing a bra that summer. How all the girls teased her at lunchtime, jealously snapping the white elastic on the back.

'Stop it, that hurts,' blushing Justine folded her arms in self-defense, feigning annoyance, 'Stop it!'

All the other girls, including Josie, couldn't wait to get their first bra, wanting to be grown up, like Justine. They all gossiped about boys at lunchtime. Who was gorgeous, who was ugly and who they'd like to kiss. It was delicious and they'd fall back on the grass bank, laughing with anticipation. John Maxfield was a favourite fantasy, the shy sandy-haired captain of the first fifteen, who smelled like Cashmere soap and wore ironed blue school shirts that matched his eyes. Justine confessed that she'd pashed him behind the bike sheds after swimming practice. The girls could only imagine. Justine was a hero that summer with her jet black curls and dimples. But Josie knew she would never get to pash someone like John Maxfield. She knew he would want a 'clean' girl. She never felt clean, even after a long bath.

Josie didn't talk much about herself with the girls. She giggled enjoying their camaraderie but she already felt damaged, not really part of the group. What would the girls think if they knew what *he* did to her? She knew it was wrong. Why did he do that to her? She had other sisters, so why her? She wondered if she had some kind of scent and that maybe a man could tell that she was bad. She often worried about it and dreaded her grandparents' visits and the forced 'Happy Families' at Christmas.

Then one night at her Grandparents villa, she was woken from sleep and realized she was being carried to her grandfather's bed. It was late and the house was still. She could hear the big Grandfather clock in the hall chiming midnight. In the bedroom the yellow streetlights, shining through the Venetian blinds, cast eerie shadows on her sleeping Nana's face.

Nana, please wake up. Look what he's doing. Help me. Wake up! Josie screamed in her head. But Nana was fast asleep. Josie could see her chamber pot under the bed and heard her snoring softly.

Then she could feel his man thing slide in between her legs and heard HIM whisper, "Ssssh don't wake Nana, good girl."
Why me, she thought, *why did he have to pick me?*

When the family got back home after that holiday, she couldn't fall asleep at night. She tossed around, feeling bad and worried that she might be pregnant. Was that sex when he did that? She hadn't had her first period yet but could she still be pregnant? The thought of being pregnant to her own grandfather, made her feel nauseous. Imagine what the girls at school would think of her. They'd think she was dirty, damaged *goods*. They already gossiped about girls who were 'damaged,' giggled and pointed at the bad girls who went with boys in the village. 'Common sluts' the girls would whisper from the bus when they'd see Shirley and Marilyn hanging around the milk bar smoking, their hair pulled back tight into pony tails and loads of make up.

It was summer when Josie turned 12, that she knew she had to put a stop to *it*. She had her first period and her Mum showed her how to put on a sanitary pad. She totally refused to go to her grandparents' house for the holidays.
'Why not Josie? You always like to go to Nana and Poppa's. Your sister will be so disappointed.'
Josie held on. It felt good to say no. 'I just don't want to go, Mum. I just don't want to! "Why not dear, why don't you want to?'
Josie ran to her room, wrapped her eiderdown quilt around her and closed her eyes, letting her imagination take her away from them all. Inside her warm cocoon she could do anything,

go anywhere. She was falling, falling, tumbling through space, weightless like the first astronauts, falling. She could see the earth below her, coming clearer. She did that a lot now, drifting off like that. Her mother would wave her hands in front of her face.

"Wake up dreamer."

Yes Josie liked her dream world better than her real world. *He* wasn't allowed in there. *He* was *banned*.

Her mother's voice seemed far away and puffy like cotton wool in her ears. "Wake up darling, you're such a dreamer."

Josie was happy she'd stuck to her decision not to go to her grandparents that summer. The relief was refreshing and she slept well those first few nights, falling into bed, sun burnt and happy after a day at the baths with her friends.

One afternoon she was pushing Maeve on the swing set Daddy had given them for Christmas. It had been fun. They had had to follow this long string, which started tied to the Christmas tree with a note:

> Follow this note to the end and
> you will find what Santa sent.
> SANTA X

The girls had run laughing, following the string out the front door, past the weeping peach tree, around the side of the house and there it was, a brand new swing set!

'Guess what kids?' Daddy strode over in bare feet and a towelling short set, quite the rage at the time. 'President Kennedy was shot today. It will most likely be World War Three.' He took a long swig of his cold one and wandered back to the comfort of the front room and the loud black and white TV.

The swing swung slowly to a stop. Maeve's legs dangled

limply. The girls stood for a minute's silence, heads bowed. Josie knew that was the right thing to do when a president died and Maeve copied everything her big sister did. Neither of them knew what it all meant or how it all affected them. Josie thought JFK was so handsome and she was sure he would smell nice like John Maxfield, even better, and he was such a loving father. She felt like crying out there on the neatly mowed lawn with the cicadas and the warm Hawkes Bay sun. She slumped down on the lawn, rocking herself into dreamland.

Maeve shook her out of it. 'Josie, wake up. Guess what? Nana and Poppa are coming here for the rest of the holidays!'

No, no! Josie screamed inside. She felt sick. *Why did he have to pick me?*

His concern was obvious when they arrived. Poppa studied her, seemed upset, but gave her the 'silent treatment.' He hardly spoke to her. Josie avoided his stares and sat close to Nana on the piano stool. She was safe there. She loved it when her Nana played the piano. The way her body rocked from side to side as she played all the World War I songs with style.

'Green, green, grass of home,' Nana sang sweetly.

Josie like to turn the page for her, following the words and singing along safe next to Nana's warm rocking arm, safe for now.

Poppa spun around as Josie was leaving to go to the baths. He was outside the garage, waiting to catch her, she thought.

'So you know all about sex now, eh?'

She avoided his eyes, looked down and studied some sticky tar on the driveway.

'Just want to be with all your girlfriends now do you?'

Josie didn't answer. She ran down the sixty-three steps, free falling away from that face, the leathery hand and that feeling: Shame.

It was many years later, when Josie herself was a grandmother, before she was able to come to terms with what affect her grandfather, the paedophile had had on her life and unfortunate choices she had made with men. Thinking herself unworthy, damaged, and always that shame eating away, making her stomach hurt, punishing her. She'd chosen men who didn't know how to treat her well, and she'd accepted that just as she'd numbly accepted her Poppa's abuse all those years. Many times she had run from these men, sometimes putting herself and her children in dangerous situations, not caring for herself and not feeling worthy of somebody good. She had refused to go to her grandfather's funeral. She felt good about that, glad that he was gone from her world forever.

'It wasn't your fault,' Anna, the round-faced councilor, smiled warm and genuine from the stuffed couch.

It was towards the end of Josie's first year of counselling for the abuse. Now aged 52, she had lived alone for fifteen years. After two failed marriages and several relationships, she preferred to live alone. Her grown children now lived overseas.

'It wasn't your fault, Josie.'

Josie's tears streamed warm down her cheeks.

Anna went on, 'You were only a child, the grown-ups should have protected you from all that.'

Crying felt good. Josie hadn't cried in years, she always held it in. Crying hadn't helped much in the past. Nobody comforted her anyway.

Anna passed her some tissues and reached over to hug her.

Her arms embraced Josie like her old eiderdown and she began falling again, falling inside. This was more like a release, giving her shameful burden to someone who listened and didn't judge.

'Thank you Anna, I want to go home now.' Josie put on her coat to go.

'Call if you need to talk.'

Josie nodded but knew she probably wouldn't.

Her old car started up and Josie turned on the radio. An old 50's tune, *Be My Baby tonight,* filled up the car. Josie could feel happiness trickling into the space inside that had opened up when she cried. She felt forgiven and now she had to forgive herself, but she couldn't ever forgive *him.* She would try and she could start over, maybe even find a good man to love, *maybe.* Josie turned on the car lights and headed for home, humming softly, *'be my, be my baby tonight.'*